Sto

DEAD LETTERS

DEAD LETTERS

SUSAN KIMMEL WRIGHT

HERALD PRESS
Scottdale, Pennsylvania
Waterloo, Ontario

Library of Congress Cataloging-in-Publication Data
Wright, Susan Kimmel 1950-
    Dead letters / Susan Kimmel Wright.
        p. cm. — (Dead-end road mysteries; 3
    Summary: While trying to figure out who is responsible
for stealing mail from nearby mailboxes, Nellie allows
outward appearances to lead her to suspect a high school
dropout, an aging actress, Sasquatch, and a lonely
classmate.
    ISBN 0-8361-9036-X (alk. paper)
    [1. Prejudices—Fiction. 2. Christian life—Fiction.
3. Mystery and detective stories.] I. Title. II. Series.
PZ7.W9587Dd 1996
[Fic]—dc20

                                                95-38092
                                                CIP
                                                AC

DEAD LETTERS
Copyright © 1996 by Herald Press, Scottdale, Pa. 15683
        Published simultaneously in Canada by Herald Press,
        Waterloo, Ont. N2L 6H7. All rights reserved
Library of Congress Catalog Number: 95-38092
International Standard Book Number: 0-8361-9036-X
Printed in the United States of America
Book design by Jim Butti/Cover art by Matt Archambault

06 05 04 03 02 01 00 99 98 97 96 10 9 8 7 6 5 4 3 2 1

Acknowledgments

Thanks are due to Edna Mae Specht, a fellow writer and clerk at the Blue Bell Auction, Stoystown, Pennsylvania, for providing the inspiration for Nellie's adventures at the auction.

Dedication

In memory of a special cousin and friend, Gordon L. Kimmel, trusting Romans 8:38-39.

Contents

DEAD LETTERS

1

Crash of the Number Two

When the school bus skidded, it threw Nellie into the corner of the backseat. Rick fell against her, squooshing the words out of her mouth in one gust. "And I said—hey!"

The bus jerked to a halt; Nellie's head struck the window with a painful thunk. "Ow!" She touched the tender spot as Rick inched back to where he belonged.

Bus Number Two tilted into the roadside drainage ditch. Kids began picking themselves out of the aisle, most laughing and talking.

"I'm sorry, Nellie." Rick's dark eyes looked worried as he reached out to check her head. "You got a bump."

"It's nothing. What happened?"

"Some jerk driving a delivery truck came barreling out of the Lucky Clover Trailer Court entrance and nearly hit us. Mrs. Hagen slid in all the slush."

Their driver, tiny and round in a purple ski jacket, was coming back the aisle, making sure everybody was all right. Even her frizz of gray curls looked alarmed.

She bent down to talk to Rick's brothers, Billy, Jeff, and Larry. They were ten, nine, and seven, in contrast to Rick's fourteen. All three were hooting with laughter. Apparently, if getting out of school at 10:00 a.m. for a broken water line was exciting, a bus accident only made things all the more thrilling.

Mrs. Hagen reached the back. "Everyone okay here?"

Rick's friend, Fred Umbaugh, nodded. "Yeah. Rick's a good cushion."

"I had a soft landing, too," Rick said. "But Nellie got thunked."

"It's okay," Nellie hastily added. "Really."

Mrs. Hagen's hands still shook as she pushed them into her pockets. "Good. Well, I guess I'd better see how much of a pickle we're in here. Richard, would you please come with me? Everyone else please remain in your seats."

Nellie, who'd jumped up to follow, reluctantly sank back down. "Phooey."

Fred grinned across at her, nodding at the forward seats. "You sound like them."

All down the aisle, little kids jumped up and down, yelling, "Let me come, too!" and "I helped my dad once!"

Nellie grinned back. "Oh, I know. But how come Rick gets to go and we have to just sit

12

around like lumps?"

"Mrs. H. may need somebody else to go call for help while she stays with us. She can't have ten kids running around out there and maybe getting hit by a car."

Nellie couldn't argue with that, but she still didn't like it. She rubbed a spot on the steamy window and squashed her nose against it for a look. Both Rick and Mrs. Hagen were staring at the ditch, shaking their heads.

"Oh, come *on*," Kathy Bauer complained from two seats up. "I'm fifty feet from home."

Nellie, usually not a fan of Kathy's, had to agree. "All the kids from the trailer court are as good as home now," she whispered to Fred. "Even the rest of us could just walk the rest of the way faster than this bus is going to get us there."

"Some of us, anyway," Fred admitted, and Nellie winced. She was such a dummy. Although he'd lost a leg a couple years before, Fred did so well on the artificial one that she never really thought about it anymore.

Warming sunshine had turned two days' worth of snow to muddy slush. Now she realized slipping and sliding down Dunkard Road wouldn't be the easiest thing for Fred.

"I'm sorry. I don't know where my brain is."

Fred grinned again. "That's okay. You did just get a blow to it."

Rick came back the aisle, his cheeks windburned. He reached for his books. Over the

13

screams of the younger children, shoving and bouncing behind him, he asked Nellie, "Want to walk?"

"Can we?" She was already on her feet.

"Sure. Mrs. Hagen said as long as we call and our parents say okay. She called for help, but this bus isn't going anywhere till help comes."

Nellie grabbed her books. "Great. Mom won't care. After all, we used to have to walk it everyday when there were only three of us and they wouldn't run a bus on our road."

Fred opened a book. "I might as well do my math. I can be done by the time you guys get home. See you tomorrow."

Nellie made a face. She had the same problem with math that she did with history—too many numbers swam in her brain and wouldn't stay put. Rick and Fred had ninth-grade geometry. She doubted she'd survive next year when she hit it.

Emerging from the overheated bus into the wind, Nellie pulled up her collar. "This soft stuff is going to freeze tonight."

She watched Kathy Bauer mince her way toward the Lucky Clover entrance, along with a plodding fourth-grader and his sophomore brother. Three kindergarteners danced through the slush. Nellie rarely saw them since they normally rode the early bus home. Already their mothers were coming out to meet them.

"Kathy's the only one I really know," Nellie mumbled. "And I hate to ask to use her phone."

Rick didn't have to ask why. Kathy somehow never missed a chance to pick on Nellie.

"We can call from Mike's," Billy said, pointing at a sturdy-looking boy walking up the steps of the first trailer. "He's in my class."

"Sounds good to me," Nellie agreed. "Go ask him."

Billy exploded into a run, kicking up slush. "Hey, *Mike!*" Larry and Jeff trotted after him.

Nellie held up hands to shield herself from the spray. "That kid's a human firecracker. He should be the redhead instead of me."

Rick grabbed her icy fingers in the cozy warmth of his gloved hands. "Nope. We Kepplers all have dark mops—family rule. You'll just have to hang onto your famous carrot top."

Nellie, who occasionally practiced writing "Nellie Keppler" in the back of her tablets, hoped they'd change the family rule by the time she grew up.

Billy had caught up to Mike at the mobile home door. It seemed to be the only one on the street without a wreath or a picture of Santa. Mike was frowning as Billy chattered in his face.

"I don't know," Mike said as Nellie and Rick approached. He fingered a key dangling from a cord around his neck. "I'm not supposed to let anyone in the house when Mrs. Lodge isn't here."

"I understand," Rick told him. "Maybe you could call for us."

Mike's rosy face looked relieved. "Yeah, I guess I could."

He watched with serious brown eyes as Rick wrote the numbers on a sheet of paper and handed it over. Rick explained the message.

"Okay. Wait here a minute." Mike fumbled with the key, then quickly slipped inside and shut the door with a tinny clank that shook the trailer. Nellie heard the lock click.

She raised her eyebrows.

Jeff and Larry were already busy trying to build a snowman on the small patch of front lawn. It kept slumping down into a tired-looking volcano shape.

Billy swung from side to side, holding the step railing. "Mike's mom doesn't live with them," he explained. "His sitter usually gets him on the bus in the morning and meets it in the afternoon. He's strange."

"Billy." Rick's voice was warning.

Billy made a face and jumped from the steps to land with a splash. "I know; I know. But I see him walking along the road all by himself. He's just—different."

Soon Mike returned. "Your moms say okay. Just don't 'dillydally.' "

Nellie rolled her eyes. She'd heard that before.

"You going to be okay here?" Rick asked.

Mike nodded, unruly brown curls bouncing. He was already slipping back inside. "Yeah. The office called Mrs. Lodge. She's coming right over."

"Want us to wait with you?" Rick offered. "We could tell our moms."

16

"No; it's all right." The door shut again and the lock clicked.

Heading down the walk, Nellie glanced back. She was sure she caught a glimpse of a brown eye and a curly forelock at the edge of the front window before they vanished.

"Poor kid," Rick said.

Billy popped up beside him. "His mom ran away. She probably didn't want such a strange kid."

"Billy." Rick's voice was weary. "Don't say stuff like that. It can really hurt people."

"Well, it's true," Billy mumbled. He took off after his younger brothers.

"Watch for cars!" Nellie automatically called after them, even though Dunkard Road was even quieter than usual in the deep gray slush.

A township truck was parked in front of the school bus now, and the driver was talking to Mrs. Hagen. Nellie waved, but Mrs. Hagen didn't notice.

The Lucky Clover trailer court sat at the civilized end of Dunkard Road. Its big, peeling green clover sign sprouted just a few feet beyond the notice that read, "Rough Road Ahead—Local Traffic Only."

Years ago, in the days of horse-drawn farm wagons, the road went through to Begg City. Now hardly anybody drove farther than Nellie's family's old farmhouse, a mile and a half down the road.

Between the Lucky Clover and Nellie's house

were the Umbaugh farm, then a tumbledown house and barn that didn't look much better than the "clubhouses" Nellie used to make when she was a little kid. Next came Kepplers, then a stretch of woods.

It was going to be hard walking in the soft snow. Nellie's boots skidded with each step. Maybe Fred was the smart one after all. She pulled out her gloves and stuck them on.

Rick's brothers were already climbing around the ditch beyond the trailer court mailboxes. The boxes were stacked in rows like mouse condos, with sprays of pine and red velvet bows on top.

"Rick, look!" Larry yelled, waving something. He sloshed back toward them, and as he came nearer, Nellie could see he was holding a wrapped stick of gum.

"Where did you get that?" Rick asked.

"On the ground. It's still wrapped; can I eat it?"

"No way." Rick peered up ahead where the boys were scrambling over the snowy ditch. "What is all that?"

"Mail, I guess," said Larry, taking off again with the gum still in hand.

"Nellie, look." Rick broke into a trot. "There's stuff all over the ground."

2

Dead Letters

The snowy ditch was decked-out for Christmas—red envelopes, green envelopes, cards with angels, photos of kids in front of decorated trees. Above it all, the red postal flags stood at attention, giving the mailboxes the look of a ragged platoon of tin soldiers, saluting their inspecting officer.

"Oh, man," Nellie breathed. "What happened?"

"Looks like somebody was tearing up the mail—maybe stealing it." Rick skidded to a stop and blew a shrill whistle at his brothers. "Don't touch anything else!"

He grabbed Jeff and Larry by their sleeves. "Billy, get up here."

The mail lay scattered in the ditch and along the road and bank beyond the boxes. Footprints marked the soft snow at the base of the mailbox posts. Nellie bent down for a closer look.

"Did you guys walk around the boxes here?" she asked.

"Nope. We wanted to check out the stuff in the ditch."

"It looks like somebody just started grabbing envelopes and ripping them open." Nellie pointed at the strewn mail. "And when he threw stuff down, the wind carried it up that way."

"Looking for money in Christmas envelopes, probably." Rick started hauling his brothers back toward Mike's. "Guess we'd better report this."

"I'll stay and keep an eye on things here," Nellie said. "Just in case."

For an instant, the younger boys hesitated, then seemed to decide calling the police was more exciting than standing in the ditch. They whooped as they went, as if this day just got better and better.

Nellie bent to squint at the envelopes. The stamps weren't canceled. People from the trailer court must have just put them in the box for today's mail pickup.

A sharp gust of wind caught Nellie in the face and swirled a couple cards farther up the road. "Uh oh!" She glanced back at the Lucky Clover, where Rick and the boys approached Mike's driveway. A scowling woman with faded brown hair was getting out of a small blue car.

Must be Mrs. Lodge, Nellie thought. Till they explained everything to her and got the police over here, the papers could all blow away.

Nellie figured she didn't have much choice. She pursued the scuttling papers, catching at the corners with gloved fingers so she wouldn't smear any fingerprints.

Sliding them into the pocket inside her notebook for safekeeping, she walked back toward the mailboxes. A baby picture, wet from slush, clung to one of the posts. And there—Nellie pounced—was a check.

As Rick had said, somebody apparently was just opening envelopes and tossing out everything but money. Somehow he'd missed this check for $25. The memo in the corner said, "Merry Christmas from Grandpa."

What a rotten thing to do. Nellie looked up to see Rick and his brothers coming back, along with Mrs. Hagen, the township worker, and a handful of other people, including Mike.

"Don't touch anything," Nellie warned. "Fingerprints."

"And better stay back from the boxes," Rick added. "In case the footprints mean something."

Except for a couple kids, who needed to be reminded to stay away, everyone stood along the bank. The grownups all talked at once.

"Can you believe it? Right in Chestnut Grove."

"It took me four hours to do my cards—just so some—"

"Well, I never put money in the mail. But I was sending my Aunt Bet a nice hankie and a lavender sachet."

"At *Christmastime*, for goodness sake!"

Nellie strolled along the road. Unless they had an accident to investigate, the police would soon be here. She wanted to see what she could before they got here.

Those footprints, for instance. She hunched down and squinted at them. Different sizes and shapes overlapped. Only a few clear prints stood out, but one was awesome.

The solitary print was about as big as one of Petrone's hoagies. It was apart from the rest and headed away from the mailboxes to disappear into the gray slush of the roadway. She couldn't see any distinctive tread markings in the melting snow.

"What are you looking at, Nell?" Rick whispered in her ear.

"That great big footprint."

"It's not very clear." Rick raised his hands and stalked toward her like a TV late-show monster. "It could even be Sasquatch."

Nellie rolled her eyes. "That's Frankenstein you're doing. Sasquatch slumps his shoulders."

Rick grinned and bowed to her superior knowledge of monsters. "Right, as usual. Anyway, this kind of sloppy snow changes fast."

"Most of them are just mush," Nellie admitted. All the same, her eyes darted from the prints to the cluster of feet on the bank. She wondered if any were a match.

Rick was right—it was useless.

Soon a young policeman pulled into the trailer court entrance. He parked in the first driveway, then walked back toward the crowd. Even with a heavy, fleece-lined jacket over his uniform, Nellie recognized that well-rounded figure. It was Slim, Chestnut Grove's own defender of justice.

Larry ran to meet him. Nellie hid a smile as Rick groaned. "That guy's going to earn his money today, if he has to interview Larry."

As it turned out, Larry was only part of the problem. So many adults and kids had come looking for excitement that Nellie could see it was going to be tough knowing who to question and who to tell to shut up and go home. Even Kathy Bauer had come to stand along the edge of the crowd, obviously straining to catch all the details.

The policeman started with the boys. Larry explained how they'd discovered the scattered envelopes. Rick translated and moved him along when he wandered into telling about the gum and how it was still wrapped but Rick wouldn't let him have it, and how his grandma couldn't chew bubblegum anymore because it stuck to her dentures.

The crowd came nearer. "Excuse me. Officer, can I tell you about my mail?" a woman asked. "I was sending five dollars to my nephew, and I need to know if it's missing."

Slim held up his hand. "*Please*, everyone. Just wait your turn."

Nellie opened her notebook. "I'd better give

23

you this stuff. It was blowing away, so I picked it up."

As his face darkened, she hastily added, "I was real careful about prints. And there's a check in there that the thief must've missed."

He accepted the stack and riffled through it. "These guys don't want checks. Only cash."

"What guys?"

He shrugged. "These mailbox crooks."

"May I look through that?" asked the woman who was worried about her five dollars.

"Please, ma'am. Just wait. I'll be with you shortly."

"Does this happen very often?" Nellie asked.

"Not usually—but this is our second one in just a couple days. It's Christmas. People mailing money." He shook his head at such foolishness. "Not very much in most cases, but tampering with the mail is still a federal offense."

He looked at Rick and the boys, then Nellie, with a stare that was probably supposed to be scary. She wondered if they were suspects and arranged her face into an innocent expression.

Larry tugged at her jacket. "Are you sick, Nellie? You look funny."

"No, of course not. Everything's fine," she muttered. Why did little boys—who ordinarily wouldn't notice if she was dying right in front of them—immediately get all loudly concerned the minute she tried to fade into the background?

Slim scratched his head with the end of his pen. "Uh, by the way, shouldn't you all be in school right now?"

24

Rick explained about the water pipe and pointed at the bus, still sitting in the ditch. "We live farther down the road, so when the bus slid, we decided just to walk it."

"When did you arrive at the trailer court?"

"Ten-twenty-five," Mrs. Hagen called down.

The officer looked around at the people on the bank. "Did any of you put mail out this morning?"

A few hands went up.

From the people who'd put envelopes in the boxes, it soon became clear when the mail thief had to have struck. The boxes had appeared untouched until sometime between the last mail deposit at eight and the boys' arrival sometime after ten-thirty. Slim scribbled in his notebook. Then he slid back down the bank to study the foot and tire tracks and examine the scattered mail.

Finally the evidence had been collected and he returned to his car. The crowd began wandering away, still muttering about "Grinches" and "five dollars" and "Aunt Bet."

"Well, now we have to call home again and explain why we dillydallied," Nellie said.

They looked around, but Mike was already gone.

3

Move Along!

Away from the trailer park, Dunkard Road looped up and around rolling hills and fields draped in patchy snow. Nellie and the boys laughed and slid as they went.

The Umbaughs' red-brick farmhouse stood back a few yards from the road, behind white fences. Beyond ranged the dairy barn and three smaller outbuildings. The driveway had been cleared of slush.

The mailbox flag was up. Curiously, Nellie looked inside. A stack of envelopes appeared untouched. "Well, I guess even crooks don't venture back Dunkard Road."

Rick grinned. "Even Sasquatch only goes as far as the trailer court."

Larry was falling behind because he was trying to practice walking backward, but Billy and Jeff started to laugh. "We saw his footprint at the mailboxes," Nellie explained.

"Really?" Jeff's voice was eager. "Some scientists think they might be real. Like cold-weather gorillas."

"I doubt it." Rick shook his head. "Where would they hide in a place like this?"

"Back in the woods." Jeff's voice made it seem obvious. "How many toe-prints were there?"

"You couldn't see toes, honey. It was too melty." Nellie grinned at Rick over Jeff's head.

Jeff, who watched nature shows instead of cartoons, never noticed her amusement. "Or it could have been a bear, I guess. Sometimes people do see a black bear around their yards. There was one at a bird feeder in Chestnut Grove just last spring."

Then he shook his head. "But they really ought to be hibernating by now."

"Maybe it woke up," Billy suggested.

Jeff looked doubtful. "Maybe." He looked at Rick. "Could you see any claw marks?"

"Nope."

"Oh, well." Jeff shivered happily. "It *could* have been a bear. Or Sasquatch."

Billy looked ahead, where trees crowded the road. "Maybe it's watching us now."

"Yeah, probably," Nellie agreed. "Or maybe he already got beamed back onto the mother ship."

"Nellie!"

"I'm kidding, Jeff."

"It's not funny. It's neat to think maybe there's something wonderful right out there somewhere—just out of sight."

She knew what he meant. "I'm sorry. I didn't mean to make fun of you."

The wooded area marked the edge of Umbaugh's property and what had once been the next farm. According to Fred, it used to be just a tree line along a scrubby pasture. In time, though, the pasture had sprouted trees and the trees grew into real woods. Even in the winter, with the leaves down, you couldn't see far back because of all the furry dark hemlocks.

As they slogged along, Nellie shifted her books to rest her aching arms. She glanced at the surrounding woods, where an occasional darting bird fluttered its wings against the silence.

Maybe Jeff was right. Even with all the deer in these woods, she never saw them unless they came out to graze or cross the road. What if there *was* another animal in there? One with the intelligence of a gorilla. One too shy to come out.

By the time they left the woods, the little boys had already forgotten Sasquatch and were discussing Christmas. The next place was little more than a shack, set back from the road, with a small weathered barn sagging beside it. Gray smoke rose in a wavering column from the crooked chimney.

Thick vines of wild grape and poison ivy crawled over the rusting wire fence, pushing it to the ground. Nellie looked beyond, across the stubble-pegged fields of melting snow. Two sets of tire tracks crawled up the driveway, though there was no sign of a car.

"What a lonely place," Nellie said.

Rick paused beside her, watching as the wind caught gray cloud curtains and pulled their shadows over the ground. "I don't know how the old lady gets by," he said. "She and her animals just keep to themselves."

"Look!" Jeff pointed. "There's a goat on the porch."

Sure enough, the mournful-faced creature was staring back at them, its front hooves planted against the unpainted railing. "Maa-aa!" it bleated.

"Maa-aa!" the little boys called back, and the goat answered.

At the chorus of goat noises, three dogs emerged from the direction of the barn. They were scraggly, wild-looking animals with matted, dirt-colored fur and thin sides. Planting themselves in front of the steps, they began to bark and howl.

"Oh, man! I think they want us to leave," Nellie said, backing away from the fence.

The front door opened; a towering figure stepped onto the porch. It looked like they'd interrupted Paul Bunyan just as he was dressing up to dance "Swan Lake." Nellie blinked. Despite the flannel shirt and overalls, it must be a woman, she decided, considering the clutch of floppy white feathers riding a crest of spiky gray hair.

"Shut up, once!" the woman bellowed in the dogs' direction. Then she frowned, focusing on

Nellie and the boys. "Move along; move along!"

The dogs, momentarily silenced, chimed in with a new flurry of barks. Even the goat maa-ed noisily.

"Sorry, ma'am!" Rick called. "We're going."

Nellie tried to trot, but her heavy boots dragged in the glop. She felt the woman's sharp eyes prodding her back.

The little boys hurried, skipping around Nellie and giggling. "Old Mrs. Move-Along," Larry muttered between giggles. "It's all she ever says."

"Have you been bothering her?" Rick asked.

"Of course not!" Billy was indignant. "I like the goat. And sometimes we look for him when we go by. That's all."

"But she always says, 'Move along; move along,' " Jeff complained. "Like we're doing something wrong."

"Who is she?" Nellie asked, wondering that she'd never cared before. No name or number marked the crumpled mailbox.

Rick grinned. "Chlorine LaFontayne."

"Huh?" Rick rarely teased her, but that name had to be a put-on.

He crossed his heart. "I kid you not. She came here from California a couple years ago. Place was empty for a long time before she moved in. Sometimes Fred and I used to camp out there."

"In the house?"

"It was almost like outside. There was a bat colony in a closet upstairs."

"Aww, neat!" Jeff said, popping up beside him.

30

"They really were. Like someone had left pairs of soft leather gloves hanging on the wall."

"Did you ever talk to her?" Nellie asked, slowing down as the house receded in the distance.

Rick grinned again. "Only once. Fred and I didn't know she'd moved in, and we went for a picnic by the springhouse in back."

"And she caught you?" Billy's eyes were big.

Rick nodded. "Came out with a shotgun. I guess that was before the dogs. We fell all over each other, apologizing."

"What did she do?" Nellie couldn't imagine facing down a shotgun barrel in that desolate farmyard.

"Told us to move along."

The little boys snickered.

Kepplers' farm came next. Shaggy red-and-white Herefords browsed through mounds of hay behind sturdy wire fences. The murky pond between them and the barn was rimmed with a crusty scallop of ice.

Billy, Jeff, and Larry started running again. "Jay's here!" Larry yelled at the sight of the battered purple Volkswagen beetle next to the house. Rick's cousin, Jay, was a high school dropout who shaved his head except for a stringy red-blond ponytail on top.

"C'mon in and warm up," Rick said, tugging at her arm. Nellie followed but slowed as she trudged up the muddy driveway to the white frame farmhouse.

The door slammed as the little boys burst inside. Nellie hesitated at the green-painted steps. "Maybe I'll just keep walking."

Rick looked puzzled. "You can at least stop for a minute, can't you?"

Nellie softened, meeting his pleading dark eyes. "I ought to get home," she said, but her feet shuffled closer to the steps.

"Just for a minute?" He pulled at her hand.

"Oh, I guess. Okay." Nellie returned the quick squeeze he gave her fingers. She'd just stand inside the door and say "Hi."

The narrow entryway was carpeted in dark red with big roses. The boys' wet boots and jackets lay tumbled at the foot of the coat rack in the corner.

Rick sniffed. "Vegetable soup. Hi, Mom!"

Mrs. Keppler appeared in the kitchen doorway. Tall and thin with a tumble of dark hair, she looked like just the mom you'd pick for Rick. The amazing part was that when he'd been just a baby, someone *had* picked her to be his mother, and the Kepplers had adopted him.

"Hi. Nellie, come on in and have some lunch. I'll let your mother know."

"Thanks, Mrs. Keppler, but I'd better keep walking."

"Oh, but Jay's here. He had a grocery delivery out our way and now he's heading back to see your mom."

Before Nellie's frenzied brain could come up with a good excuse, Mrs. Keppler called, "Jay! You can run Nellie home after lunch, can't you?"

Nellie tried not to look desperate as Jay ambled through the doorway. He was wearing a small reddish mustache these days, but his face seemed more boyish than ever.

"Sure, Aunt Deb. Hiya." He smoothed a hand over his "Make Mine Pepperoni" T-shirt from Petrone's Pizza.

"Uh, hi, Jay. Thanks, but I'd better get going and work on my homework."

"I'm running back there, anyway," he mumbled, but Nellie thought she'd seen a flicker of relief in his brown eyes.

"I'll tell Mom you're coming. She'll be glad to see you," Nellie told him. Strangely, it was true. Mom had taught Jay's Sunday school class a few years back and she always said he was a "dear boy." She'd drop everything to sit and talk to him on the rare occasions when he came by with one of his never-ending problems.

Jay kind of ducked his head in a way that could have meant "thanks," "bye," or "see ya," and slipped back into the kitchen. Jay only used words when there wasn't a grunt or gesture that would convey the general idea.

"No lunch then?"

"No thanks, Mrs. Keppler. I've got to be going. See you tomorrow, Rick."

"Maybe. Unless the water line's still broke."

Nellie brightened. She hadn't really considered that possibility.

A raw gust caught her face as she stepped back onto the porch. Nellie drew her neck down into the collar as she zipped her jacket.

She thumped down the steps and squished past Jay's VW. As usual, the car mystified her the same way he did. Ancient, battered, and impossibly purple, it looked like a giant bruised plum.

But inside—she bent to look—it was all clean and shiny. No dirt, no fast-food wrappers. A blue-and-purple afghan covered the driver's seat.

The corner of a white plastic bag peeked from underneath a seat. Nellie guessed he even hid the litter bag.

She straightened and continued down the driveway. Slogging another mile through cold and slush was definitely unappealing. And without Rick and the boys it was strangely quiet.

The road, leading off into the woods ahead, seemed lonely and unwelcoming. Nellie glanced back at the warm house where Jay sat with his car keys, before setting her face toward Sasquatches and bears and walking on.

4

Watcher in the Woods

Nellie was beginning to wish she'd stayed on the bus. Her boot was rubbing her left heel and she tried to shuffle so it didn't get worse.

Beyond Kepplers' fields, the woods closed around the road once more. She'd have to walk with the shadow of the trees cold on her shoulders for more than a half-mile. After that lay her own house and the surrounding fields.

These were real woods—logged out decades before the Great Depression but left to grow dense ever since. When Nellie was seven, they'd moved to the rundown farm on Dunkard Road. She'd done a lot of exploring as a little kid, but never far into those woods. She knew, from talking to Rick and Fred, that the trees rambled way down to Dunkard Creek and climbed the bank on the other side. The only paths were deer trails.

Not much sunshine hit the road surface, even with the leaves down. Few cars tackled the dirt road, either—especially when it was mucky, which was most of the time.

As a result, the snow lay deeper here, though soft and pitted by drops from the overhanging branches. Nellie's leg muscles had started to ache. So had her arms. She stopped a moment to shift her load of books.

As she paused, the cool air brushing against her cheek, she felt another sensation, like a prickling at the back of her neck. It was a feeling like being invisibly watched.

When her family moved into their house, it had been standing empty for a long time. It wasn't until she'd started second grade that fall that she'd heard the rumors that their house was haunted, as well as the Dunkard Church ruins beyond. Nobody would walk this stretch of road alone.

She hadn't really believed the stories, of course. But still she'd heard more noises at night after that. And she hadn't liked being alone, either, especially when she was in bed and Mom and Dad were still downstairs.

A little of that feeling came over her now. How long had it been since she'd walked along this road alone?

Big baby, she told herself, stepping faster. There were just trees and animals out there, and the distant rushing of the creek.

What was it that made a lonely road seem scary—even for people who really truly didn't believe in ghosts? "The Lord is my shepherd," she whispered. "I shall not want."

She hadn't gotten to "even though I walk through the valley of the shadow of death" when she heard it. Just a single snap, like the breaking of a small branch, but the way it cut through the still air made her look back.

Nellie jumped. Someone was standing in the hemlocks several feet back from the road.

She could just make out the shape of a head and one huge shoulder in the darkness between the trees. *No*, she told herself over the frantic pounding of her heart. *I'm imagining things.*

Where would a hulking stranger have come from, after all? There was no sign of a car, no footprints along the road but her own.

Nellie backed away, still staring at the motionless figure between the trees. *Could it be a bear?* Jeff had been right about people reporting seeing them, but not very often—a cub here or there. And they might have been imagining things, too.

Besides, nobody had reported a bear sighting since last spring, when the hungry critters had been emerging from hibernation. So probably her eyes were just playing tricks with shadows.

Trying not to think about a news story she'd read, of a bear attacking a wilderness hiker out west, Nellie closed her eyes. When she opened them, she'd see nothing but trees.

But when she opened her eyes, Nellie saw two other eyes looking back at her. They were red and glowing—and really high up. She screamed.

37

5

Jay's Troubles

Any thought that she'd imagined the figure vanished when Nellie screamed. Whoever—or whatever—it was whirled and fled, the hemlocks closing like a dark curtain behind it.

Shamelessly, Nellie ran the other way, her boots clomping as she bolted for home. Despite all the sticks on the ground under the trees, the escaping figure was much quieter than she was.

By the time Nellie had rounded the next bend and clattered over the narrow wooden bridge, she was too breathless to run anymore. She looked nervously over her shoulder at nothing but trees and snow-covered road. Still, she hurried as much as she could, not daring to stop.

The sight of the farmhouse brought a relief so great, she felt weak inside. Its peeling paint and the curl of gray smoke from the cookstove chimney looked beautiful against the tarnished red of the barn.

As Nellie passed below the little graveyard on the hill, she heard Lady's muffled bark. Somehow the dog always knew—even from indoors—when anyone was coming.

The kitchen door opened and a mass of brown fur rocketed across the yard, leaped the ditch, and charged up the road. "Hi, girl." Nellie reached down to greet her friend.

Suddenly Lady skidded to a stop. She sniffed the air, looked suspiciously at Nellie, and growled.

"Lady, what's the matter?"

Uneasily, the dog backed away. "I wish you could tell me what I smell like. Maybe then I'd know what it was I saw."

By the time Nellie reached the kitchen door, she was feeling self-conscious. Lady stalked just behind her, occasionally slipping in close enough for a quick sniff at her heels. Every time she did this, a growl rumbled deep inside the dog's throat.

Nellie went through the door and collapsed against it. Lady edged away with a wild-eyed backward glance and a grumbling noise in her chest.

The dog disappeared onto the sunporch, an old-fashioned, windowed family room running the length of the house. Feeling rejected, Nellie hung her coat on a peg beside the door, then leaned against the wall to tug off her boots.

Mom's footsteps padded through the hall. As

she stepped into the kitchen, she leaned over the counter that separated it from the sunporch and peered at Lady.

"What was *that* all about?"

Nellie blew her nose. "I wish I knew. Whatever I smell like, she doesn't like it." Her voice still shaky from the scare and the long run, Nellie explained about the dark figure in the trees.

"Well! You've had quite a morning." Mom turned and began pulling sandwich stuff from the refrigerator, as if she didn't know what else to say. She began layering Swiss cheese, bread, and lettuce.

Finally she looked up. "Could it have been your imagination, Nell?"

Nellie shook her head. She knew her story was too weird for her to take offense if Mom thought she'd dreamed it. "No. I didn't just see it—I heard it."

Mom poured orange juice, then pushed aside dirty dishes, the morning newspaper, and used baby bibs to clear a spot for Nellie's lunch. "What do *you* think it was, Nellie?"

Nellie plunked down and curled stockinged toes around her chair rung. "Well . . . I don't know." She pushed straying lettuce leaves deeper into the sandwich, getting mayonnaise on her fingers.

"It could've been a person, I guess. But it seemed way too tall. And there weren't any signs of a car."

"An animal of some kind?" Mom suggested.

Nellie shook her head. "Maybe. But what could be that big?" She laughed. "Rick's brother Jeff would probably say it was a bear—or a Sasquatch."

Mom plopped into the chair across from Nellie. Despite the tired lines around her eyes, she looked like a teenager in her worn sweatshirt and jeans. "Excuse me?"

Nellie giggled again and explained how they'd been talking on the way home. "I know what you're thinking," she hastily added. "But it didn't give me any ideas. I did hear what I heard and I saw what I saw."

Mom pushed back her thick, garnet-colored hair. "Well, people really do claim to have seen bears, but I don't think—well, for one thing, they'd all be asleep now. Unless, of course, something disturbed them."

She put a gentle hand on Nellie's. "Maybe it was something smaller—like a raccoon—sitting on a limb."

"Maybe." Nellie noticed that Mom didn't waste any breath on the Sasquatch theory.

As soon as she finished eating, Nellie jumped up. "I'm going to get out of my school clothes," she told Mom. "By the way, Jay was at Kepplers. He's coming to see you."

Mom jumped up, too. "Now? I'd better straighten up."

Nellie snorted. "Not for him."

"He's company like anybody else."

Nellie shook her head. Jay was like nobody

41

else the world had ever seen.

"Be quiet up there—okay? Danny's finally taking a nap, and I've got a lot I need to get done."

When Nellie changed, she put her school clothes straight into the hamper, then washed her hands. Maybe Lady would come near her now.

She tiptoed through Danny's room to get to the stairs. It used to be her room before the adoption, but now she was used to seeing it with yellow chickie wallpaper and a crib and changing table.

Nellie glanced down at his round, brown cheeks and glossy dark curls. He slept with his mouth open. Now that he wasn't teething—at least for the moment—he was getting to be almost nice to have around. She touched his back, feeling its warmth rise and fall.

"Hi, Jay!" Mom's voice rose from the kitchen. "Nellie said you were coming. What a lovely surprise!"

Nellie made a face. She shut Danny's door and tiptoed back into her room. There was a hole in her floor, covered with an iron grate, designed to let the heat up from the rooms below. Gently she lifted the wooden cover.

Lying on the floor beside the grate, Nellie could hear the voices go into the living room. She felt a little bit guilty about eavesdropping, but sometimes it was the only way she learned about things.

This wasn't one of the more exciting conversations she'd ever heard. Jay was one of those people whose problems had problems.

Apparently, he was in love with a girl named Shelley, whose dad hated him because he didn't have a high school diploma or any money. He couldn't make more money because he didn't have his diploma. He couldn't get his diploma because he still couldn't read very well. He couldn't read because he had some kind of reading disability. Plus he had no time to do much about it because he had to work two jobs—at Petrone's Pizza and the Superette—because he didn't have enough money.

After listening to him go around and around for half an hour, Nellie wondered what he wanted Mom to do. Teach him to read? Lend him money? Talk to Shelley's dad?

Still, he sounded more cheerful by the time he was leaving. And Mom had told him to put in a pizza order for them for tonight. That definitely made Nellie more cheerful.

6

Rumble at Petrone's

It was already dark when Dad and Nellie went to pick up the pizza. "I'll wait out here, Nell," he said, pressing money into her hand as he turned up the radio. "I want to hear the weather forecast."

Nellie pushed open the restaurant door to chattering voices and the smell of spicy tomato sauce. Jay stood at the back entrance in a worn leather pilot's jacket over a "McKenzie for Treasurer" T-shirt. He was stacking pizza boxes into an insulated carrier for delivery.

A waitress with a long black ponytail handed him another pizza box. Nellie couldn't see her face, but Jay grinned like a lovesick puppy when their hands brushed.

Was this Shelley? Nellie stepped up to the takeout counter and gave her name, still watching Jay and the waitress.

The girl turned back to pick up an order.

Even under the bluish glare of the fluorescent light, a pink inner glow lit her warm olive cheeks. She was beautiful, and—amazingly—she seemed to like Jay.

Nellie was squinting to read her nametag as she passed, and the counter man had to repeat himself. "Your pizza, miss."

As she counted out the money, Nellie's brain was elsewhere. So this was Shelley. What on earth did she ever see in Jay?

Nellie was just handing her payment to the clerk when something crashed at the back of the store. She looked up to see Jay on the floor by the rear door, the pizza carrier upside down beside him.

Everybody in the kitchen stared in horror as Jay struggled to his feet on a floor made slippery with escaped pizza sauce. A man with a tie—probably the manager—rushed over. He tiptoed across the pizza slick and grabbed the carrier.

"Bill! Bring a mop." He pulled boxes out onto the table and lifted a lid. It was coated with pepperoni and cheese.

"Oh, man!" He opened more boxes. "This is fifty bucks' worth of pizza, Jay."

The manager glared. "And people are waiting already, for crying out loud. What happened?"

Jay mumbled an answer, but Nellie couldn't hear what he said. Whatever it was, the boss wasn't impressed. He wiped his hands with a wad of napkins, then shoved more at Jay.

"Clean up, klutz. Marie, start calling these

folks. Let them know their pies are going to be late. Deke, replace these orders." Red-faced and scowling, the manager strode off into a back room.

Everybody else pretty much went back to work. One of the cooks—a young guy with a lot of dark hair—smirked as he bent to flatten a ball of dough. Probably Deke.

Shelley slipped past Nellie and back through the kitchen. She caught Jay's arm and whispered something.

Jay muttered in reply, gently removing her hand from his wrist. Rigid, he charged over to Deke and spun him around.

"You did that on purpose." Jay's voice shook.

Deke raised his eyebrows. "You're crazy, Klutz Man." Pointedly, he turned his back.

For a heartbeat, Jay stared at him, breathing hard. "This isn't over," he said at last. "If I get charged for those pizzas, you're going to learn to watch your big feet."

He stormed through the door—maybe to cool off while Deke made more pizza. After an uncertain glance at the amused cook, Shelley followed Jay. Nellie thought she saw tears in her eyes.

Interesting. Had Deke tripped Jay? Jay obviously thought so. Nellie wondered why.

She picked up her rapidly cooling cardboard box and headed for the door. Dad started the engine before she was even inside the car.

"What took so long?"

Nellie told him about the unpleasant scene

in the kitchen. "Even I felt embarrassed for him."

Dad turned off the highway toward home. "That boy goes around with a black cloud over his head. Growing up without a father had to be hard, but even now, it's like trouble just follows him."

Nellie watched the headlights bounce as the road dipped and curved. "What happened to his dad?"

"Divorced, I guess." Dad shrugged. "Connie— his mom—doesn't talk about it. She's been Petrone's janitor for years."

"Do they really live above Petrone's?"

"Rent's cheap. And he's probably never late for work."

For a long time, they were quiet. Nellie shifted the box on her lap. It left a warm place across her legs.

They were on Dunkard Road now, passing the lights of the Lucky Clover before heading into darkness. Dad glanced at the trailer court. "You had quite a day."

"Yeah," Nellie admitted. "Dad, what do you think I saw in the woods?"

He shook his head. "I don't know, Nell. Just where was it?"

"Up ahead here. I'll show you."

Dad slowed the car as trees closed around the road. "Okay. Along here somewhere?"

Nellie strained to figure where they were in the blackness. "Right about here, I think. I'd like to look around in the daylight, but with school and all, it's dark by the time I could get down here."

"Hard to tell anything now," Dad agreed. "Maybe it was just a deer."

Nellie didn't say anything. She remembered how big it was. The look of those eyes, the blocky shape of the head and neck. What deer ever looked like that?

"Dad?" Nellie shifted the box again. "Do you believe in Sasquatch?"

"Well-ll." He seemed to be giving it some thought. "I don't know, Nell. Let's say I don't *not* believe. There are an awful lot of reports from all over the place, that are an awful lot alike. You have to wonder. What *did* all those people see?"

"Dad?"

"Yeah?"

"Do you think—uh, do you think Sasquatch is like a-a person?"

He didn't laugh, the way Nellie thought he might. But as he pulled into the driveway, he shook his head.

"No, Nell. If there is a Sasquatch—and I don't know that there is—I don't think he's some kind of person. None of the sighting reports would suggest those creatures were acting human. And if we're made in God's image, what would that make Sasquatch?"

"An animal?"

Dad grinned and shrugged. "A mystery, Nell."

Mom had salads and cider on the table when Nellie and Dad came into the kitchen. She took

48

the pizza and popped it into the oven of the big iron cookstove to warm.

Danny sat in his high chair, chewing on his bib. "Hi, squirt." Nellie brought her face close to his little brown nose.

"See if he needs changing, will you, Nellie?" Mom asked, at the same time Dad called from the living room, "Hey, come quick!"

Nellie picked up her brother and followed Mom. Dad had turned on the TV news, and there was a picture of the Lucky Clover and its mailboxes.

The story didn't tell Nellie anything new. But after the reporter explained about the thefts, he concluded with a lighthearted interview with a couple who looked like they might be retired. They lived at the wooded edge of the trailer park.

They told how they'd arrived at the scene after the police and found some "very suspicious tracks" near the mailboxes.

"They just made us think—you know—" The woman looked at her husband. "We had to wonder because of what we saw behind the house last summer."

"It was like—" The man's eyes darted to his wife. "Like a big ape. Came out of the woods and stepped right over the fence. Three-and-a-half feet high and this thing stepped right over it."

"It was almost dark," the woman quickly added. "But still, what could just step over a fence like that? Our dog, Tiger, ran and hid under the bed."

Nellie didn't blame Tiger, a toy poodle the size of a TV dinner. But it reminded her of Lady's reaction when she'd come home that afternoon.

"Then when we saw the mail that way, and that track, we figured maybe he was curious," the man said. "You know how them apes are. Maybe he was just checking it all out and it got scattered."

Mom shook her head and started back to the kitchen. "I can't believe they wasted air time on that."

But Nellie shivered and rubbed her arms. If she closed her eyes, she could still feel the chill of those lonely woods. She could still see those strange, glowing eyes looking back at her.

7

Back in the Woods

"If you see anything, just tap my shoulder or something," Nellie murmured. "Don't say anything. Okay?"

Peggy's glance darted along the trees lining the slushy road. "Just what am I looking for?"

"A big animal, a person. Or any signs of them. Like footprints or something."

Peggy sighed. "You know you're my best friend, Nell, but. . . ." Her voice trailed away.

"But what?"

"You don't really think some ape messed with the mail, do you?"

Nellie managed to snort. "Of course not. But I saw something. I really did. And it wasn't just a deer." She crossed her heart. "And he was looking right back at me."

Peggy didn't say anything. She trudged beside Nellie, hands in pockets, and stared at the woods ahead.

51

Nellie's lips tightened. Peggy didn't believe her. She wasn't talking because she knew anything she said would just upset Nellie. Of course, Nellie knew her well enough to figure all that out and get mad.

They came to the place where that cluster of hemlocks stood back from the road. Nellie stood for a moment, listening for the slightest sound.

Nothing.

The trees looked normal—dark, shaggy, deserted. Slowly, Nellie turned, looking all around the quiet woods on both sides of the road.

Peggy stood beside her, still silent, following her glance. Finally, she pointed. "Was that the place?"

Nellie nodded. "Right in the middle of the hemlocks there. Let's get a closer look."

Peggy followed, dragging her feet. "Let's just hurry. I don't want to waste a day off from school. By tomorrow that water line's going to be fixed."

The leaf litter beneath the trees was brown and marshy. Only an occasional small patch of soft snow lay melting in the shadows, its surface spotted by flecks of dirt and dead needles.

Nellie pulled back the hemlock boughs, surprised at the way her heart hammered against her chest. Nothing unusual caught her eye.

The boughs looked unbruised and the few patches of snow were unmarked. Nellie let go of the branches and walked around the cluster of trees, studying the ground. She bent down, but that slight ruffling of the leaf surface might just as well have been the work of a squirrel.

She walked a little farther into the woods, but Peggy just plopped on a rock and waited. Finally, Nellie gave up.

"Nothing," she said in disgust. "Whatever it is, it's light on its feet."

"Probably a deer," Peggy said confidently. "They land like butterflies."

Nellie oozed back through the marshy woods toward the road. "Even they leave tracks and droppings," she muttered. "This thing might as well be a CIA operative."

Peggy giggled. Being here with her, Nellie was beginning to wonder why she'd ever panicked and run away. How silly. She should have walked right over for a better look at the time. It was just Jeff and all his talk about bears and Sasquatch that had gotten on her nerves.

Walking back along the road toward home, Nellie felt her tight muscles relax. She started telling Peggy about Jay's visit and the weird scene at Petrone's.

"You know, he could be the mail thief, Nell." Peggy's voice was excited. "It was handy—his just happening to show up on Dunkard Road right when someone's stealing mail."

"Come on, Peg. Just being strange doesn't mean he's a criminal. He's Rick's cousin."

Peggy sniffed. "So being Rick's cousin means he's something special?"

"No, but—" Nellie clamped her lips in frustration.

"You said yourself he's hard up for money. So here was a chance to pick up a few five- or ten-dollar bills, just like that. He could pull right up to the mailboxes and never even have to get out of the car."

"But he did get out, Peg. I mean, the crook did. There weren't any tire tracks next to the boxes. And the envelopes were just scattered all over the place."

"So he got out." Peggy waved her hand. "I'm just saying it would have been almost too easy for him."

Nellie tried not to think about whether Jay might have had a grocery delivery near the other mailbox break-in. Peggy was right, though. He *was* there, and he was broke. She wondered if it had really been litter in that bag stuffed beneath his car seat.

By the next day, the broken water pipes had been repaired, just in time for Nellie's most despised class—history with Mrs. Wagner. To Peggy, it was all exciting stuff. But even when Nellie tried, she just couldn't keep all those names and dates straight in her head. They didn't mean any more to her than the Latin names for species of bugs.

Wagner kept trying, though, looking for that switch that would turn on the lightbulb in Nellie's brain. Today she had a new approach.

Instead of droning through their regular assignment, Mrs. Wagner hauled out a paperback called *The Foxfire Book*. She said it started as a school project for some mountain kids who went out and talked to the old folks about the way things used to be.

When Wagner started reading, Nellie felt her jaw kind of drop. She glanced over at Peggy and some of the other kids. Their eyes were big, and Peggy grinned back at her.

Mrs. Wagner was normally the kind of teacher who worked on Nellie like a lullaby. Nellie knew she tried to be interesting, but she was a droner.

Suddenly, though, Wagner seemed to turn into another person. She became Aunt Arie—Wagner said "Aint"—a Georgia mountain woman, talking about cleaning up a hog's head for cooking.

Number one, it was really gross, especially the eyeball part. It was the kind of thing that would make Nellie's vegetarian parents throw up, and the last thing Nellie could imagine Mrs. Wagner reading.

Number two, the really amazing thing, was that Wagner *became* "Aint Arie." The way she talked didn't even sound like English, but it was pretty somehow. Listening to her, Nellie found herself getting into it and following the story.

When she was done, Aint Arie—uh, Mrs. Wagner—said, "I grew up in the mountains and, believe me, the way those people lived will never come again. Most of it isn't written in any history book. But isn't it worth remembering?"

She laid the book on her desk. "I think you boys and girls will gain a better appreciation of history if you do what the Foxfire students did.

"So for your next assignment, I'd like you to interview an older adult—maybe a grandparent—about how they used to live in the old days. I have some suggestions for you on this sheet I'll be passing around. Write up what they tell you in a typewritten report."

When they left class, Nellie walked slowly. Peggy was dancing around, planning to interview all four of her grandparents. But Nellie didn't have any nearby grandparents. There were the historical society ladies and Mr. Spangler, but they were all the way over in Begg City. Was there somebody at church?

The idea didn't hit her until she was riding home. Nellie was the last kid left on the bus as it lurched through a big pothole in front of the ramshackle farmhouse with the goat on the porch.

Nellie looked back at the lonely house, lying like a wasted fragment of gray driftwood in the middle of the barren fields. Nerves and fear joined with excitement to tighten her stomach.

Chlorine LaFontayne should have a story to tell!

8

Trouble with Rick

The next morning, Nellie couldn't wait to tell Rick. "I called her!" she said, still impressed with her own nerve.

"No kidding? Will she talk to you?"

"Well, she was a little suspicious at first, but then she decided it would be okay. At least if I could give her a hand around the place."

"You mean you have to do *work* for her before she'll talk to you?"

Nellie shrugged. He made it sound as if Chlorine had tricked her. "No, not really. It was my idea—I think. And she sounds real interesting."

"I hope so," Rick muttered. "Between the shotgun and putting you to work."

"I think she's just lonely and that old rundown place is too much for her. Besides, everybody around here keeps a shotgun to protect their livestock. She didn't actually threaten you with it."

"Well, just make sure somebody knows where you are. Maybe you shouldn't go alone, either."

Nellie's lips tightened. "Mom already talked to her, thanks. She's going to drive me over."

"Hey, that's good." Rick didn't notice her irritation. "Maybe you're right about her being lonely. Jay says when he delivers her groceries, she talks his ear off."

Fred got on the bus in front of his driveway. While he and Rick talked, Nellie thought about Jay. Jay delivered Chlorine's groceries. In fact, that must have been the delivery he'd been making on the day of the mail theft. Mrs. Keppler had said that was why he'd been in the neighborhood and stopped for lunch.

Nellie wondered when he'd passed the Lucky Clover. The mail could have been stolen any time from about 8:00 a.m. to just before the bus went into the ditch. Peggy was right—it looked like Jay had been in the right place at the right time.

She grabbed Rick's arm. "Hey, Rick. Do you have any idea when Jay got to your house the other day?"

"No, why?"

"Oh, I just wondered. If he stopped for lunch, he couldn't have been there too long, could he?"

He frowned. "I guess not."

"You sound like the cops." Fred grinned. "Is he under investigation or something?"

"Well—I wondered. That's all." The deepening scowl on Rick's face told Nellie he knew exactly what she'd been wondering. And he didn't like it.

"Jay's okay," Rick said. "He's always getting blamed, like it's his fault he's had a rough life."

"I wasn't blaming him for anything." Nellie put up her hands. "I'm only wondering."

"Wondering if he's a lowlife crook that rips open Christmas cards to steal money," Rick snorted. "Maybe you didn't accuse him yet, but that's what you're thinking."

Nellie's face felt hot. She'd never, ever had Rick mad at her, and she couldn't stand it.

She swallowed before speaking. "Rick, I know he's your cousin. I didn't mean to accuse him of anything. I really was just wondering. You know me. I can't help the detective stuff."

He didn't smile the way she'd hoped he would. "He's a nice guy, Nellie. If he'd graduated from high school and had a good job so he could dress better, people would like him. It's not fair."

Personally, Nellie thought being poor was the least reason people didn't trust Jay. He dressed weird, talked weird, acted weird. But being poor *was* one big reason to steal money.

She tried again. "Rick." Her voice came out kind of pleading. She noticed that Fred had tried to fade into the background, staring out the window so he didn't get sucked into this argument. "Try to forget for a minute that he's your cousin. Okay?"

Rick's jaw looked like he was gritting his teeth hard enough to shatter them. Finally he said, "Yes?" His voice was cool and a little sarcastic.

"Imagine it's somebody else. Somebody who can't even afford health insurance. Somebody who's in love with a girl whose dad hates him because he'll never amount to anything. Imagine he sees a chance to pick up some cash—just like that. He's right there, and there's the money."

For a moment, Rick didn't say anything. He just stared ahead and his jaw kept working. Finally, he turned back to Nellie.

"Why don't *you* imagine? Why don't you imagine that this person has some integrity? Do you think every poor person in the world is dishonest?"

"No, but—"

"But what? What makes you think Jay would stoop so low? Because I know him, and I know he never would. I don't think he'd steal a crumb if he was starving."

"I don't know," Nellie admitted. "I don't know him like you do. But—"

The bus pulled into line in front of the school. Rick stood up.

"Then maybe you shouldn't blame people for stuff you don't know anything about."

For the first time since he first admitted he liked her, Rick turned his back and walked up the aisle without Nellie.

9

The Birdwoman of Dunkard Road

Rick's anger clung to Nellie like cat hair. When she sat next to him on the bus that afternoon, he said "Hi" and listened to her talk about her day. But none of it felt right.

That old relaxed feeling was one thing Nellie loved about being with Rick. She knew other girls who had to act silly, like they were someone else, when they got around their boyfriends. But Rick had always been a real friend she could talk to. Now that seemed to be changing.

When she woke Saturday morning, the memory hit her like a sinking in her chest. She and Rick weren't the same anymore. And over something as unimportant as playing detective.

Peggy had slept over so that she could go to Chlorine's house with Nellie. Thank God for Peggy. Nellie didn't want to be alone with her thoughts. And she certainly didn't want to be alone with Chlorine, either.

Mom stopped the car at the end of Chlorine's driveway. "I don't want to get stuck in that mud and slush today. I'll just turn around here."

She looked at Nellie. "You want me to stop in with you for a minute?"

Nellie shook her head. "We'll be okay."

Peggy opened the door. They both crawled out, Nellie clutching her history notebook. As they called their goodbyes and slammed the door, they roused the dogs.

Like a hungry pack of coyotes, the dogs came around the side of the house, growling and barking. Mom paused in her backing up and waited, halfway in and halfway out of the driveway.

Chlorine emerged onto the porch in a long red robe with a feathered fringe all along the flap. "Shut up once!" she bellowed at the dogs. They sank to their bellies and looked up at the great red birdwoman with adoring grins.

Seemingly reassured, Mom pulled out, beeping the horn and waving to Chlorine. Nellie took a deep, steadying breath and started up the driveway, dodging puddles.

Peggy leaned closer. "Are you sure she's—all right in the head?"

Nellie grinned. "No. But enough people are, anyway. Crazy people are more interesting."

Through lowered lashes, Peggy looked at the figure in the doorway. "I could probably do without something that interesting," she muttered.

Nellie snorted. "Don't be a wimp." But she whispered, "Lord, please let this be okay."

As they stepped into the yard, the dogs came forward to sniff their legs. Nellie started to reach a hand to pet them but drew it back.

Burrs clutched clumps of their hair like ugly barrettes. The air around them smelled of unwashed dog and unscooped droppings.

Almost gagging, Nellie tried to hold her breath. Above them, Chlorine stood untroubled and almost queenly, one arm extended to welcome them onto the porch.

"Hello, my darlings. Come right on in."

The heady aroma of perfume wafted out to clash with the dog smells. Up close, Chlorine was as Nellie had said—interesting. The robe looked like something from a glamorous old movie, but Chlorine's feet were stuffed into gray-and-red wool hunting socks and battered barn shoes.

The porch floor sagged as they creaked across. Nellie wondered how sturdy it was; a stack of concrete blocks holding up one corner.

"Step right in," Chlorine invited and Peggy threw Nellie a despairing look.

Nellie pretended not to see. "Thanks, Mrs.—"

"*Miss*," Chlorine told her. "Miss LaFontayne."

Nellie stepped on inside, Peggy scrunching along close behind her. Chlorine's voice drifted in after them. "Forgive the clutter, my darlings. I hadn't a moment to straighten up."

A moment wouldn't have done it. No way. Not unless she had Aladdin's genie hidden somewhere in all that stuff.

Nellie stood still, trying to take it all in and

make sense of it. As long as she could remember, Nellie's house had been a mess. But next to this place, it could have been a sterile operating room.

She'd rarely seen so much stuff. The low-ceilinged room was so filled with a strange assortment of furniture, books, antiques, boxes, and indescribable clutter that if the roof fell, it couldn't have dropped more than a couple inches.

Nellie shivered. It was chilly in here. Chlorine gestured at the couch, a sagging green relic tufted with dog hair. At least Nellie assumed it was dog hair. Her ears pricked at a sound like maa-aaing from a back room. She shook her head to dismiss the craziness. Even Chlorine wouldn't keep the goat inside.

Nellie was used to a certain amount of dog hair, since Lady shed year-round. She plopped right down, but Peggy gingerly spread her jacket before sitting.

Chlorine floated to the opposite armchair and sank with a certain grace. She was still smiling, which Nellie took to be a good sign.

The spiky gray hair Nellie remembered was gone. In its place was a sleek, licorice-colored bob, crowned with a red feather.

It was obvious that if Chlorine hadn't bothered to houseclean, she had certainly put her efforts into beautifying herself. She'd used enough makeup that—as long as she stayed in the shadows—she didn't look real, real old.

Her sharp black eyes met Nellie's with a dancing expression. "So, my darlings! You're here to interview me about my film career."

"Uh—" Nellie thought fast, hoping her absolute shock didn't show on her face. "Yes. Yes, your . . . career."

The keen dark eyes grew dreamy. "Well, where to begin? Are you familiar with any of my film work?"

Nellie ignored Peggy's desperate look. "Not your earlier work," Nellie ventured. She opened her notebook. "May I take notes?"

"Certainly, darling. Well, I should imagine my earlier work *would* be unfamiliar to the younger generation. I was just starting out, you know, and so many of my roles were of a supporting nature."

"Like what, ma'am?"

"*Under Two Flags*?"

Nellie gave her a blank look. "Ah, well." Chlorine waved a hand. "Claudette Colbert got the lead in that one. They wanted a *name*, and exotic foreigners were all the rage."

Chlorine got to her feet. She was a towering woman, with shoulders like the figurehead of a ship. "Have you seen *King Kong*?"

Not waiting for a reply, Chlorine went on. "Remember the scene where Kong is on display and the crowds are gawking? Then the poor thing breaks loose and everyone screams and scatters?"

She posed, throwing up her hands and opening her mouth in a look of horror. "*I* was the girl who did this."

"No kidding? I'll have to watch for you the next time it's on."

"Poor, misunderstood and ill-used beast." Chlorine wiped her eye. "And of course, they wanted Fay Wray there. Somebody little and wispy. I was always more of a Joan Crawford/Roz Russell type."

"I see," Nellie told her, scribbling a note. She had no idea what a Joan Crawford/Roz Russell type was, but she could see where Chlorine had probably never been wispy.

For an hour and a half, Nellie took notes while Peggy, with all her allergies, was kept busy sneezing. They learned how Chlorine had left home at sixteen. "People did that back then, but don't you try it—no, sir! Things are different now."

They also learned how she'd given up the only man she'd ever loved and headed for Hollywood to pursue her "gift" and dream of stardom. She came near to success time and again. Nellie's brain swam from looking at scrapbook clippings. But somehow Chlorine remained just one of the faces in the crowd scenes and never quite became a star.

"Oh, I did well enough," Chlorine told them. "I made a living. Yes, I did. And, of course, I became known as 'the Appalachian Songbird.' We all had nicknames back then. I did sing a bit, you know.

"And of course," she patted her hair and the

feather wobbled, "I always wore feathers. It was my trademark."

Nellie tried to ignore the sounds coming from under the coffee table, but finally had to lean down for a peek. A puffy orange cat was working hard to bring up a hairball.

"Uh, what made you give up your career?" Nellie asked.

Chlorine gestured around her and smiled. "It was time to return to simpler values and a simpler life."

"I see." Nellie looked at her notes. She wondered if she could use any of this for her history paper. Maybe she should have asked some questions about old-time moviemaking.

"Well, my darlings. I'll be happy to share more with you another time. But now I'm sure you'd like a drink or snack before tackling that work you so kindly agreed to help with. Your dear mother will soon be returning."

Chlorine rose and beckoned them. "Won't you come along now?" She drifted like a great red swan through a back doorway.

Peggy looked at Nellie and sneezed tremendously. "God bless you."

Peggy blew her nose. It looked red and swollen. "She's crazy, Nellie. You'll never be able to use any of that stuff she told you."

"Shh!" Nellie glanced toward the door. "You'll hurt her feelings." She got up, pulling Peggy behind her. "We'd better go on into the kitchen."

Peggy pulled back and Nellie looked. Peggy

stood with her arms raised in front of her and her mouth wide open like she was screaming, just like Chlorine in *King Kong*.

Nellie snorted and patted her arm. "Poor misunderstood beast. Come on!"

The kitchen was a little cleaner than the living room. A bright movie poster, tattered at the edges, decorated the wall above the table. The movie was *Under Two Flags*.

Now Nellie could see Claudette Colbert, pictured next to a dashing-looking man. She wondered if Chlorine had ever been as pretty as the actress on the poster. You really couldn't tell from those faded newspaper clippings.

"Here, my darlings. Some of my own lemon balm tea." She poured from a pot nestled in a quilted cozy. "So good for the digestion."

In the brighter light, Chlorine looked like she might be eighty. Of course, if she'd really been in *King Kong*, she'd have to be old. It was hard to imagine, though, the way she flitted around.

Chlorine dumped another scrawny black cat from one of the chairs and gestured for them to sit down. She shoved overflowing cardboard boxes out of the way.

"These boxes, you see, are part of what I *so* need help with, dear girls." She sank into a chair.

"These drafty country places are so expensive to keep up, you know. Especially these winter heating bills."

Nellie's fingers felt stiff from taking notes in the chilly house. Eagerly, she reached for her teacup, but it was only lukewarm. Chlorine must have made the tea before they arrived. Nellie glanced furtively around the room, but there was no microwave.

Chlorine sighed as the black cat leapt onto the table beside her. "And of course I have so many pets to feed. So I thought, why not take some of my white elephants to the auction? Maybe I can pick up a little cash."

Nellie sipped at the tea and flinched. Could she spit without anyone noticing? Maybe it would have been better warm. As it was, the sharp lemon flavor reminded her of furniture polish. Holding her breath, she gulped it down.

Chlorine didn't seem to notice Nellie's struggles. She lifted a dented cake pan and an ugly orange dancing-girl lamp from the box. "If you girls would be so good as to transport boxes to the porch, perhaps your dear mother would take them to the auction house for me."

"I'm sure she would," Nellie agreed.

"There's more in the bedroom," Chlorine said. "Come see."

As soon as she turned, Nellie poured her tea into the sink. Peggy's followed. "It coated my teeth," she muttered.

The small bedroom was musty-smelling. Its single window let in only a faint ray of light, which fell across the tufted pink furrows of the bedspread and showed a crudely stitched mending patch near the bottom.

More boxes sat on the bed and floor. "These

all go," Chlorine said, gesturing toward the door. "Perhaps you could set them out on the porch."

"Yes, ma'am." Nellie reached for the nearest box, at the foot of the bed, then jerked away as something hissed at her.

Chlorine patted her arm and giggled. "It's only Olivier." She pointed at a puffed-up gray cat on the bed. "You disturbed his nest."

Shakily, Nellie picked up the box. "Follow me," Chlorine told her. "I'll open the door."

The box wasn't all that heavy, but was so big Nellie couldn't get her arms all the way around it. Near the top, she could see old mayonnaise-jar lids, an ashtray, and a rug of braided plastic bread bags. She staggered toward the door with her awkward load, then scrambled to set it down as the bottom began coming apart.

"Oh, dear." Chlorine waved a hand at Peggy. "Perhaps you'd better handle that one together."

Peggy set her box back down and came to slide her hands underneath Nellie's carton. "Do you have any package tape?"

Chlorine shook her head. "Sorry, darlings. Can you manage?"

"Yes," Nellie grunted. "We'll just take it this way."

They shuffled out through the tight corner by the refrigerator. Nellie's glance snagged on a school photo stuck to the refrigerator door. What was Chlorine doing with a picture of Mike?

10

Sasquatch!

By the time Nellie and Peggy dumped the last boxes onto Chlorine's porch, it creaked under the weight. If Mom didn't bring the big old station wagon, Nellie realized, she'd never be able to take all this in one trip.

"How'll we ever get this stuff up to the road?" Peggy muttered.

"Slowly," Nellie told her. "And a lot of trips."

Peggy groaned and rubbed her back. "It's slippery out there, too. We'll be lucky if we don't land on our seats."

"I know." Nellie's arms ached. "We'll just have to do the best we can."

"Girls!" Chlorine's lilting call came from the doorway. "You've worked so hard. Won't you come in for some more nice, warm tea?"

Peggy gave Nellie a desperate look. "I'm just getting feeling back in my tongue," she hissed.

"Coming!" Nellie called, then whispered to

Peggy, "Maybe she'll turn her back again."

Peggy still hesitated, scanning the road for some sign of Nellie's mom. But when the big tan goat suddenly scrambled up the steps and onto the pile of boxes, she made a quick decision. Hustling so he couldn't follow, Peggy squeezed through the door behind Nellie.

"Maybe I should call Mom now," Nellie suggested at the first whiff of tea rising from the pot on the kitchen table.

"Nonsense," Chlorine sniffed. "You girls deserve a little rest after all that hard work."

Reluctantly, Nellie sat down. Chlorine poured generous mugsful for each of them. It was steaming; she must have made it fresh.

Taking the chipped mug in her hands, Nellie prayed for inspiration, anything to distract Chlorine before she had to drink this stuff.

The kitchen window faced an overgrown pasture and weathered barn. Dense woods crowded against the far pasture fence.

"Miss LaFontayne?" Nellie hesitated. "Do you believe in Sasquatch?"

She half-expected her to laugh, but Chlorine's eyes grew bright and interested. "Why, it's strange you should ask that, my dear. But, my goodness! Yes, I've seen him several times." Her glance traveled to the window.

"You've . . . seen him?" Peggy asked.

Chlorine nodded, then rose and floated toward the window. Unfortunately, the sink was right beneath it.

Well, Nellie hadn't touched her tea, so it wasn't like there were germs in it. Quickly, she lifted the lid of the pot and poured her tea back inside.

Chlorine didn't seem to notice the faint clink as Nellie replaced the lid. Instead she was pointing toward the treeline. "Once last summer, the dogs set up a terrific racket. It was just at dusk and, being all alone here, I checked it out right away."

Peggy was wide-eyed, so caught up in the story she forgot herself and took a big gulp of tea. Nellie stifled a snicker as Peggy gagged, gasped for air, and started coughing.

Chlorine didn't notice. She was clearly reliving that summer night. "I came to my bedroom window for a look. No air conditioning, either."

Chlorine chuckled wheezily. "So the window was open. The dogs were near the corner of the barn. You can just about see from here. They were barking toward the treeline, but they wouldn't go any closer.

"Just that quick—" Chlorine snapped her fingers. "I saw it. It was a big thing. Like a man in a gorilla suit, but much bigger. He stood at the edge of the woods, then just like this he steps over the fence, coming this way."

Chlorine stepped daintily, showing how easily the creature had cleared the fence. "The wire's a good four feet high," she added. "No man could step over it like that."

"Then what did it do?" Nellie asked.

73

"He kept coming," Chlorine said. "The dogs didn't scare him. In fact, he headed right for them. He had a long stride." She stretched out her arms. "And he covered that pasture like nothing.

"Well, the dogs ran for the barn door, but by then I was spooked, I tell you. And I don't spook easy. So I picked up my shotgun and aimed for the dirt in the backyard. Boom!"

Peggy jumped, sloshing tea. Nellie poked her, partly to let her know she was being silly, but mostly to cover Nellie's own jump.

"The thing took off then. Three steps and it was over the fence and into the woods."

"Did you hit it?" Peggy asked.

Chlorine laughed. "Shoot, girl! A shotgun don't have that kind of range." Her voice lapsed into a sort of hillbilly twang that hadn't been there before.

"Did you ever see him again?" Nellie asked.

Chlorine shook her head. "No, my dear. Not since then. But I see the occasional track. Yes, I do. And once, earlier, I saw him moving along the fenceline—just a shadow, mind you, but it couldn't have been anything else." The twang had disappeared.

She wandered back toward the window. "Sometimes I feel it was a mistake to shoot. Perhaps he was trying to contact me."

Peggy muffled a snort. "More likely he was trying to make contact with the garbage can," she muttered.

11

Mysterious Tracks

Snow fell overnight, erasing dirt and slush. When Sunday dawned, it was like a blank page, still waiting for its story to be written. But temperatures rose all day, darkening the coating of white and melting it to slush again.

Nellie got on the bus Monday morning with anticipation thumping at her throat. Rick's family had been away Sunday, and she wondered if he was still mad.

"Hi, Nell! Did you get your 'exclusive interview' with Chlorine?"

She grinned with relief, hearing the old easy tone of voice that said all was forgiven. "Hi! Sure did. Hey, you didn't tell me she was a movie star."

"A *what*?"

"A movie star." Nellie grinned again. "Didn't you know? She almost got the part of King Kong's girlfriend."

"You're kidding."

"Nope. That was almost her in *Under Two Flags*, too."

"Under what?"

Knowing things were all right with Rick made Nellie want to keep them that way. If she made him laugh, maybe they could forget last Friday. She imitated Chlorine, telling him about her "career" and shielding her face in terror when Kong escaped. Nellie didn't really intend to make fun of Chlorine. She just got carried away.

Next thing she knew, she was telling him all about Sasquatch "trying to make contact." She crooked an elbow over her eyes and sobbed, "poor misunderstood beast!"

At first, Rick looked like he wasn't sure how to react. But Nellie's impression was so funny, he soon started laughing. Especially when she suddenly shifted from feeling sorry for Sasquatch to blasting at him with an invisible shotgun.

"One thing for sure—you'll have the most interesting paper in class," Fred told her.

Nellie's face fell. "I can't put that stuff in my paper. Who's going to believe all that crazy stuff about Sasquatch and being in the movies? Or even that her name's Chlorine?"

She was starting to feel bad about making fun of Chlorine. The old lady couldn't help being lonely and kind of crazy.

Nellie felt worse when she saw Mike looking at her. He didn't usually ride their bus, but today he was there and his face was angry. Nellie remembered his photo on Chlorine's fridge.

Her cheeks grew warm and she looked away. She felt like she did when she ate too much junk food or watched something bad on TV. When she gave in to something wrong, it sat like cold lumps in her stomach afterward.

"Well, she did have scrapbooks, didn't she?" Rick asked. "That would prove the movie business, wouldn't it?"

"I guess." Nellie shrugged. "I want to go back and help her out some more. Maybe I can figure out something I can use."

During the next week, Nellie carefully said nothing to upset Rick. She also decided Chlorine's story of seeking her fortune in California during the Depression was interesting. If Mrs. Wagner didn't believe it, that was too bad.

Sunday brought a surprise. Rick caught her in the basement hallway before Sunday school. "Did you see the paper?"

Nellie hung her coat on the row of hooks, then draped her scarf over it. "What paper?"

"This morning's newspaper. It made the front page."

Nellie shook her head. "What?"

His eyes danced with laughter. "You'll never believe it. They found Sasquatch tracks at Chlorine's yesterday."

"No!"

He nodded. "She called the police and they called the Pennsylvania Center for UFO Research."

Nellie stared, afraid Rick was teasing her and she was falling for it. "UFO research?"

"Yeah, apparently that's the group that investigates these things."

Mr. Dietz, the Sunday school superintendent, came down the steps. He smiled and said "Good morning" as he passed, but his look reminded Nellie they'd better get in to their class.

Coming home from church, Nellie looked out at Chlorine's farm. There were a lot of cars in the driveway, including a blue van with a TV station logo on the door. People carrying cameras milled around the yard.

"Hey, can we stop?" Nellie asked, ready to grab the door handle.

Dad kept driving. "No. We're going to eat our lunch. Your friend obviously has her hands full of tourists already."

"Maybe later?" Nellie asked hopefully.

"We'll see."

That was as close to a promise as she was likely to get; Nellie knew better than to push it. She sank back against the seat, turning her head to watch the excitement at Chlorine's house until it disappeared from around the next bend.

By the time lunch was over, though, Dad had decided *he* wanted to go to Chlorine's. "How many chances does a guy get to see Sasquatch tracks?" he asked.

Mom raised her eyebrows.

" 'There are more things in heaven and earth, Horatio, than are dreamt of in your philosophy,' " Dad told her.

"Don't throw Shakespeare at me," Mom said. "You're just being nosy."

Dad grinned and shrugged. "I prefer the term 'intellectually curious.' "

"I'm sure you do." She turned to lift Danny from his baby seat.

"We'll be back soon," Nellie promised, grabbing her coat before Dad could change his mind.

"Here," Mom said. "Don't forget this." She handed Dad the camera.

Things hadn't quieted down much by the time Nellie and Dad arrived. The TV van was gone, but a radio truck had replaced it. Neighbors still trooped around the yard, laughing and talking.

"Shall we announce ourselves?" Dad asked.

"I guess." Nellie hung back to let Dad go up the steps first. There was no sign of the dogs. Maybe Chlorine had penned them in the barn, with all these visitors.

Dad knocked on the warped door and flakes of paint floated down. "Remind me to come back and see if this lady can use a hand with something," he said.

Nellie didn't say anything. Dad couldn't even keep up with their own place, and it needed paint, too.

The door opened and a strange man with a beard looked out. "Yeah?"

Nellie craned her neck to see past him. "Excuse me. I'm a friend of Miss—"

"She's in an interview right now, hon. You'll have to wait."

Nellie could see Chlorine enthroned on the couch in her red gown and feathers. A photographer was snapping her picture while a woman took notes and another man held a microphone.

"He's reaching out to me," Chlorine told them, flinging out her arms. "Perhaps there's a message he wants desperately to communicate."

She was involved in her role and didn't notice Nellie and Dad. "That's all right," Dad whispered. "Maybe we'll stop back later."

He cautiously walked down the steps, then bent to look under the porch to see what was holding it up. He shook his head.

Nellie followed as he walked around behind the house. There was a yellow police tape strung along the sagging length of barbed wire that separated the pasture from the yard.

People milled along the barrier, laughing and pointing. A woman in a red jacket squatted on the sloped roof of the little springhouse, adjusting her camera focus.

Rick and Fred were standing near the barn, beside Fred's father. "Hey, Nellie!"

She trotted over. "Hi." Dad came behind and shook Mr. Umbaugh's hand.

"She ought to sell tickets," Dad said. "This is a bigger deal than the Firemen's Carnival."

Mr. Umbaugh laughed and pointed, herding Nellie and Dad in front of them, so they could see. "There they are, along the fence and back."

Nellie leaned over the tape and looked. The tracks came from somewhere behind the barn, approached the fence and returned.

The prints were as long as a good-sized zucchini. They were broad across the toes and about as far apart as Nellie's head and feet.

"They're not very clear," she said. "But it looks like four toes."

Rick pointed. "You can see toes in the print nearest the barn. But the way the snow's been melting, they'll soon be gone."

Nellie moved closer to the barn and looked. "Where do they come from?"

"They think up in the woods there. But there are too many bare patches to be sure," Fred said.

The long, brown pasture grass was only splotched with soft snow. In many places, rocks jutted above the grass. Probably the shadow of the barn made this spot cooler, so there was more snow on the ground right here.

"Well," Nellie reasoned, "tracks should still show up on the grass. Sasquatch is supposed to be real heavy, and the ground's soft and wet."

Rick shrugged. "It depends. Maybe when the tracks are fresh, but these are getting old."

"I guess they already tried following them back into the woods," Nellie said. "There should still be snow under the trees."

"Hey!"

The voice at Nellie's elbow made her jump. Rick's brother Jeff looked up, face shining. "Hi! You know what, Nellie? Some researchers think

Sasquatch tries to walk where his tracks won't show—like on logs and stones and stuff."

"He isn't human, Jeff," Nellie said, then added, "if he even exists."

Jeff glared. "Animals that hunt by their sense of smell will try to hide their own scent. So if another animal, like Sasquatch, hunts by sight, he'd probably try not to leave tracks."

"Okay, Jeff. I see what you mean."

"Did you take a look on the other side of the barn?" Fred asked.

"Couldn't see much," Jeff told him. "That darn yellow tape goes all the way across."

"I'll bet you could get up to that spot along the tree line by coming up through the woods from the road," Nellie said.

"You're as bad as Jeff," Rick told her. "Forget it. Besides, Chlorine would probably turn the dogs loose or blast you with her shotgun."

Still Nellie thought she could do it. She sighted along a straight line, from the last track she could see to the edge of the trees.

If she came up from the road, just following Chlorine's property line, she'd come right to the fence. Then she could just follow that. Chlorine wouldn't mind if Nellie told her first.

Nellie turned back to explain it all to Rick, then stopped. Mike was sitting on Chlorine's back step, holding the scrawny black cat.

His eyes, meeting hers, glittered with something like contempt. Then he dropped his glance to the cat and stroked its fur.

12

A Big Discovery

The Sasquatch story died down with the melting of the snow. The next Saturday, Nellie tried to get back through the woods to track footprints, but the undergrowth was too dense.

Besides, she grumped to herself, *the snow's all gone now, anyway.*

That night Nellie was sleeping over at Peggy's. First they went to a movie, then walked to Petrone's to eat pizza and wait for Peggy's folks to pick them up.

Petrone's parking lot offered a shortcut from Melrose Street to the restaurant. As they crossed between rows of cars, Nellie saw Jay's purple plum-mobile a few spots from the side door.

"Hey, look. Jay left his lights on," Peggy said.

"He was probably coming back from a delivery and daydreaming about his problems." Nellie slipped between the cars and tried the driver's door. It was unlocked.

"Well, where are the lights?" The switch wasn't in the same place as on their car.

She slid into the driver's seat. Squinting at the dashboard, Nellie patted all around until she located the right button. The orange brick wall of the building in front of her went gray as the headlights clicked off.

"Okay," Nellie said, sliding back out. "Let's eat."

As she swung her legs down, papers fluttered to the wet pavement. "Oh, darn. My heel got caught in the litter bag. He must have still had it stuffed under the seat."

Peggy was already peeling scraps up from the asphalt. "Here." She shoved them at Nellie. "Just hold open the bag."

Obediently, Nellie stuck it out. She watched absentmindedly as Peggy stuffed papers and envelopes back inside.

It was only after everything had been picked up that Nellie realized what she'd seen. "Hey!"

She looked up quickly to make sure no one was coming. Then she reached into the bag and pulled out a damp wad of paper.

"Nellie!"

"Just a sec. I think—" Nellie held an envelope to the light so the return address was visible. "Oh, man."

"What?"

"Look. Where do you think Jay got this?"

Peggy bent her head to read. " 'Emerson. 859 Belmont Ave.' I don't know."

"No, no. The return address. 'Huffman, 12A Shamrock Circle.' "

"Well, he's not either of those people."

"I know, but listen," Nellie said impatiently. "Do you know where Shamrock Circle is?"

Peggy shook her head.

Nellie glanced up at the door again, then back at Peggy. "That's the Lucky Clover Trailer Court. And look at this."

She held the envelope so Peggy could see. "The stamp was never canceled."

Peggy frowned. "So you think —"

"He must have stolen this from the mail at the Lucky Clover," Nellie said.

Peggy took it, hands shaking, and looked more closely. Nellie reached back into the bag and checked other envelopes.

"None of these are Jay's."

"What about the stamps?"

"See for yourself." Nellie fanned them out so the uncanceled stamps showed.

Peggy shoved her envelope back at Nellie. "Put them back, Nell. Quick, before somebody comes out."

Nellie stuffed everything back in the bag and slipped it under the seat. She shut the door and stood facing Peggy under the floodlight. The harsh white beam washed all the color from Peggy's face. Or maybe finding the stolen mail had already done that.

Nellie realized they were both breathing like they'd been running. She took a slow deep breath. "Look, we've got to pull ourselves together and act natural when we go inside."

"We can't go inside now!"

"We have to," Nellie told her. "We have to call your parents like we promised."

"Okay," Peggy said reluctantly. "But I can't eat anything."

"You've got to," Nellie insisted. "We can't just go in there and hang around by the door and try not to look at Jay."

"I'll throw up."

"No, you won't. Come on." Nellie strode toward the front door, not looking back. When she pulled it open, Peggy was behind her.

The restaurant was dimly lit and noisy, with video games near the entrance. Behind the crowded dining room was the take-out counter and a hallway that led to the side entrance, the rest rooms, and a pay phone.

Nellie gave Peggy a little shove. "Go call your folks. I'll get us a table."

"Jay's behind the counter," Peggy hissed.

"Could you yell that a little louder? Go ahead —act natural."

Peggy wove her way across the dining room. Nellie found a table near the front door and slid into a seat. She draped her jacket over the chair back, watching as Peggy approached the counter.

Peggy rushed past Jay, darting him a nervous look before escaping into the hallway. Nellie groaned. Jay had seen her. Nellie wondered if she'd had the wits to say "hi."

Just as Peggy slipped into the hallway, she collided with someone coming the other way. Nellie could hear the "oof" of surprise all the way across the room.

Peggy disappeared. Nellie hoped she was headed for the phone.

The person she'd hit came into the kitchen. Nellie could see over the counter that Deke was wearing a jacket over his cook's apron.

He hung it on a peg and said something to Jay with a sarcastic grin. Jay's face turned redder than the "Cherry Blast" soda pop can on the front of his shirt, and Nellie could see him mutter something.

It was late for a cook to be arriving. The sauce stains on Deke's apron told Nellie he'd already been at work for a while.

She started to tremble. Had Deke stepped outside for a break? If so, he'd have been standing in the shadows near the side entrance. He couldn't have missed seeing Nellie and Peggy rifling through the stolen mail from Jay's car.

13

Information for the Police

Nellie sank in her seat, eyes darting from the rear hallway to the kitchen area, where she saw Deke working, back turned to the dining room.

She gave Shelley her order, without even thinking, then stuck her straw in the Coke she'd brought. If Deke had seen them, what would he do about it? Tell Jay?

Nellie shook her head. Surely not. She'd seen enough the last time she was here to know the two hated each other.

And Jay hadn't even looked this way. As she watched, he put on his jacket, then stacked several pizza boxes in a carrying pouch and headed for the door.

Just then Deke turned. Automatically, Nellie ducked, spilling her drink and scattering ice cubes across the table. "Stupid!" she fumed at herself, crouching beneath the table. She might as well have jumped on the table and yelled.

Soda pop cascaded over the table's edge like a dark, sticky waterfall. Nellie stayed down, pretending to mop at it with her napkin.

"Good grief, Nellie!"

She recognized Peggy's shoes.

"Is Deke looking over here?"

"Who's Deke?"

"Never mind. Is *anybody* looking?"

"Everybody," Peggy said cheerily. "There's a busboy coming with some rags and a dustpan."

Shelley was with the busboy, carrying a damp rag for the table. Nellie had to get up then, but she shrank into the entryway, between the jukebox and a video game.

People had gone back to their pizzas, as far as she could tell, and Deke was turned around and twirling dough in the air. When Shelley and the busboy left, Nellie wiped her chair with a napkin and sat back down.

"Are your folks coming?"

Peggy nodded. "In half an hour. Who's Deke?"

Nellie explained. "Peg, I don't know what to do. I can't face Jay. And how would we ever explain going through his stuff?"

"But if I just report him, he'll hate me." *And so will Rick*, she thought.

"Well, we can't just ignore it," Peggy said. "Somebody who rips open Christmas mail is no good. We can't just let him get away with it."

"No, I guess not." Then Nellie brightened. "But maybe if Deke *was* watching, he'll report it. Then we don't have to get involved. He and Jay can't seem to stand each other, so I don't think he'll mind turning him in."

"Well. . . . Maybe we could wait a couple days and see."

"Exactly," Nellie said, feeling a small wave of relief.

By Wednesday morning, the newspapers still said the police had no clues to the mail robberies. Nellie felt like she couldn't even lift her feet onto the bus steps.

She'd decided she'd talk to Rick today. Surely, when he heard about the envelopes hidden in Jay's car, he'd understand why she had to come forward. Rick would know what to do. If he wasn't Jay's cousin, Rick would have been the first one she'd talk to about this.

It was hard to find words to begin. Finally she took a big breath and started talking. Seeing Rick just looking at her, she felt like she'd jumped out of an airplane and wasn't sure her chute would open.

Whispering, she explained about Jay's headlights and about the litter bag falling out. "And when we were stuffing it all back in," she concluded, "we saw a bunch of envelopes from the Lucky Clover. They were all ripped open. And the stamps hadn't been canceled yet."

Rick's face darkened. "Come on, Nellie. Don't try to explain. At least admit you were investigating. You found your evidence, so be happy."

"But I wasn't—" Nellie sputtered. "I was just—

Rick, I wouldn't lie to you. And I'm *not* happy. I'm miserable. I wish I'd never found those envelopes."

Rick grabbed her arms and looked intently into her eyes. "Then forget it, Nell. There has to be another explanation. There has to be. Jay would never steal."

"But, Rick—" Nellie swallowed. Was he asking her to cover up for Jay? "How can I forget what Peggy and I saw with our own eyes?"

"He's a neat freak, Nellie. He probably found that stuff and just picked it up. If you report it, he'll be in all kinds of trouble, and he can't take anymore of that."

"Well, he'd get a chance to explain," Nellie said. "If he had a good explanation, it would come out."

"Ha. Nobody's going to believe a high school dropout who looks like a mugging suspect."

"That's his choice," Nellie said. "He doesn't have to look like that. And nobody told him to drop out of school, either."

"You don't know what his life's been like, Nellie. Jay never fit in at school. He's really a nice guy, but he never could sit still for class. He was born restless, and his brain isn't wired right for schoolwork. I think he felt like a freak for so long, he finally decided he might as well look like one."

"That's stupid," Nellie said stubbornly. "That never makes anything better."

"So when do people always do what makes sense? I think he'd been hurt so many times, it was like his way of saying, 'I don't care and nothing you do or say is going to hurt *me*.' "

"Rick, lots of kids have trouble in school. They don't just give up and expect the world to feel sorry for them." Nellie didn't want to argue; she just wished Rick could see the other side.

"That's just it," Rick said. "He doesn't expect you to feel sorry for him. He doesn't expect anything. You think he should be able to take hold because you've always had a mom and dad to back you up. Jay's dad was a bum who ran out on them. And Aunt Connie had to work to support them, plus try to help him through school."

Nellie didn't say more. She did feel sorry for Jay—a little. But if he was stealing mail, it certainly wasn't the right way to deal with his problems. And Rick didn't even seem to want to believe it *might* be true.

She slouched in her seat. She couldn't talk to Jay. She just couldn't. But if she just reported him, how would he react? Nellie shuddered. She knew how Rick would react.

She watched the morning traffic slide by the steamed bus windows. If only she hadn't found those envelopes. But now that she had, it made her responsible. If she didn't report what she knew, she'd share the blame if he stole again.

When Nellie got home that afternoon, she dialed the phone before she had a chance to lose her nerve. A voice answered, "Police."

"I can't say who this is, but I have—uh—information about the mail thefts."

14

A Rotten Day

Nellie smelled the warm metallic breath of the heater when she woke and heard its gentle ticking. The air was cold, nevertheless, on the arm she cautiously stretched outside the quilt.

She had a bad feeling inside, as if she'd done something wrong. While she dressed with fumbling fingers, she prayed, "Please let everything be all right."

Smells of burnt toast and the clatter of pots came from the kitchen. In the corner playpen, Danny sat squarely on his diapered bottom, banging two pans together. Mom was at the table, pouring juice.

"Morning," Nellie mumbled, sliding into a chair.

"Oh, I could just explode." Mom set Nellie's glass down hard, sloshing juice. She wiped her hand.

Nellie looked sideways at her.

"There must be a terrible mistake," Mom said. "The radio news just said Jay's been arrested for those mail thefts. That poor kid! They have him in jail—with criminals."

Nellie gulped. She hadn't really expected them to throw him in jail. She'd just thought they'd question him.

"Well, they must have evidence," she ventured.

"I don't care," Mom said. "It must be a mistake. Jay would never steal. Never."

Nellie didn't know what to say to that. As she ate her breakfast in silence, Mom kept talking. "I have to call Connie. I wonder if she'll be able to afford bailing him out. Maybe we can help. Oh, this will just kill her."

It was evidence, Nellie told herself fiercely. *He was practically caught red-handed. I couldn't just pretend I never saw it.*

But a little voice answered, *You should have talked to Mom. She would have told you the right thing to do.*

Nellie realized she'd had her hands clamped over her ears as she rested her elbows on the table. She pulled her hands away, but Mom didn't seem to notice. She must have thought Nellie was just resting her sleepy head.

Maybe I can just tell her now, Nellie thought. *She'll know what to do.*

But as Mom stomped around the kitchen, mixing baby formula and muttering about a "cowardly anonymous tip," Nellie found her tongue wouldn't work. Mom was hardly ever this furious.

"It'll work out," Nellie said lamely.

"Things never work out for that boy," Mom said, stowing bottles in the refrigerator.

"Oh, Nellie." She turned and caught Nellie's shoulders. "Pray for Jay today. He needs all the help he can get."

Uncomfortably, Nellie looked away. "Sure, Mom."

Mom kissed her and gave her a quick hug. "I love you. Now get going, or you'll miss the bus."

Nellie collected her jacket and books. She pulled her hat down over her ears. But she dragged her feet.

If she missed the bus, Mom would drive her to school. She wouldn't have to see Rick till lunchtime.

She plodded up the hill toward the mailbox, Lady yipping at her heels as if to hurry her. Nellie stopped beside the sprawling winter skeleton of the lilac bush, heaving a sigh that made a cloud in front of her face.

Nellie could already hear the approaching school bus. If Mrs. Hagen saw her, she'd wait.

It was no use. Even if Nellie hid, Mom would see the bus and know she'd missed it on purpose.

Eyes focused on her feet as they shuffled through the dirty wet snow, Nellie trudged on to the stop.

When Rick boarded the bus, Nellie tried to read his face. But he never met her eyes. Before he reached the backseat, he turned his back and sat down, two rows ahead.

Nellie swallowed. He knew she'd done it—or he guessed. And he wasn't giving her any chance to talk about it.

She turned her face to the steamed window, resting her cheek against her fist. It was going to be a rotten day.

15

Worse News

By Friday night, Rick still hadn't spoken to Nellie. Unless she counted that "How *could* you?" when they'd passed in the hallway. He hadn't waited for an answer, though, so it was hardly a conversation.

After seeing how Mom and Rick acted, she hadn't even told Peggy she'd been the snitch. She just couldn't take one more person acting like she was rotten.

Peggy had chattered through lunch both days, wondering who'd tipped the police and why Jay did it and what she and Nellie should do on Saturday. Nellie mostly grunted, which was enough to keep Peggy going.

But by Saturday afternoon, Nellie decided she needed to talk. She and Peggy were sprawled on the Penwicks' sand-colored living room carpet, working on their math. Actually Peggy was working. Nellie was worrying, eating potato chips, worrying, and picking tinsel fragments from beneath the Christmas tree.

Peggy's cat, a fat lilac-point Siamese named Penelope, knocked down another shower of tinsel. She narrowed her eyes at Nellie and blinked. Even Penelope was acting superior.

Nellie stuck out her tongue. "Hey, Peg."

"Huh?"

"Can we talk?"

"Sure." Peggy kept scribbling.

"I feel awful," Nellie admitted. "Everything's wrong."

"Like what?" Peggy looked up.

Nellie rubbed at her face, trying not to start crying. "Like Rick hates my guts."

"Don't be silly," Peggy said, crawling over and giving her a hug. "Rick doesn't hate you."

"Yes, he does." Nellie gulped. "All because of that stupid Jay."

"What's Jay got to do with it?"

"Everything." Nellie fished in her jeans pocket for a wad of tissue and blew her nose. "He blames me because Jay's in trouble."

Peggy's jaw dropped. "That's crazy! Why should he blame you? Jay's the one who stole stuff, and somebody reported him. So how's that your fault?"

"For reporting him."

Peggy frowned. "Why would he think you did it? I think it was Deke. You said he hates Jay. And he probably saw when we found the mail."

Nellie shook her head. "Because I *did* it, okay?

98

Deke didn't call the cops; I did."

"Oh." Peggy sat back on her heels.

"And Rick thinks I'm a rat and so does my own mother. Just for doing the right thing."

Peggy looked like she was thinking. So did Penelope. "Well, Deke probably reported him, too. Or he was waiting to see if you did, first. It was bound to come out. I still don't see where you did anything wrong. If the guy's a crook, he has to be turned in."

"They don't think he *is* a crook," Nellie said. "Rick figured he drove by, delivering Chlorine's groceries, and picked the envelopes up from along the road 'cause he's a neat freak."

"Well, he could tell the police that's what happened."

Nellie shook her head. "Mom talked to Mrs. Hostetler—his mother. She told her Jay didn't know *how* those envelopes got into his car."

Peggy raised an eyebrow. "That's dumb. Who's going to believe that?"

"Probably nobody." Nellie leaned back against the couch. "But that's just it. Anybody who's going to lie could come up with a better excuse than that."

"So you think it's the truth?"

"I don't know! I wish we'd just left his stupid headlights on."

Peggy swished her ice cubes and took a drink. "Well," she said finally. "Isn't that kind of 'it?' Jay's the type of guy who forgets about his headlights and couldn't even finish school. He's riding around with evidence in his car. Why would you expect somebody like that to think up a slick excuse?"

Nellie looked out the window at tiny snow-flakes swirling in the air. She wanted to believe Peggy, but—

"Mom and Rick say he isn't dumb."

"Oh, come on."

"No, really. He has some learning disabilities, but they say he's really intelligent."

"He's got some way of hiding it, then."

Nellie shrugged. She couldn't argue with that. "Anyway, they let him out of jail. Mom wants me to stop at Petrone's and give him a note from her and Dad. I think they're offering to help him."

She made a face. "Peggy, how can I face him?"

"He doesn't know anything."

"No, but I'll still feel funny."

"Well, at least he never says anything. It's not like you've got to carry on a conversation or any-thing. Just give him the note and split."

"I guess you're right," Nellie mumbled.

"Here," Peggy said, scrambling to her feet. "Let's not wait till suppertime. I don't feel like Petrone's tonight, anyway."

She shoved her books under the couch with one foot. "We'll just go deliver your note and get it over with. Dad's supposed to run to the hard-ware store sometime this afternoon. I'll just ask him to take us along."

Nellie jumped up. It would be great to be done and leaving Petrone's. She didn't think she'd ever eat there again.

Petrone's in the middle of a Saturday afternoon was strangely quiet. Two ladies sat talking in a corner booth, and Shelley was refilling all the napkin holders.

"Excuse me," Nellie said. "Is Jay here?"

"He ain't here!" called Deke, coming from the cooler with a huge log of white cheese over his shoulder.

"Will he be in tonight?" Peggy asked.

Shelley's dark eyes brimmed with tears. The cheese landed on the table with a loud thunk. "He don't work here anymore. Try upstairs," Deke said, jerking his thumb toward the ceiling. "Outside steps."

"He don't—er, he doesn't?"

"Nope." He whacked off a hunk of cheese with a cleaver, dark satisfaction showing on his face.

Shelley, who hadn't said a word, mumbled, "Excuse me" and fled into the hallway. She grabbed her coat and purse from a wall hook.

"That's my shift. I'm leaving now," she called into the kitchen.

"Hey, wait up!" Deke said, abandoning the cheese. "You forgot your present."

He dashed into the hall and pushed a small box in red gift paper at Shelley. "Merry Christmas."

She looked down at it like it was a bad math grade. "Thanks." She shoved it into her purse without meeting his eyes, then turned and stumbled over his big feet.

"Easy, Shel." Deke caught her and held on longer than he had to.

She pulled away. "See you Monday."

"Will you miss me?"

"Like a rock in my shoe."

"Ha, ha," Deke said, but he wasn't laughing.

"Well," Peggy said.

Nellie and Peggy's steps clanged up the steel stairway from the parking lot. Jay's car wasn't in the lot, but Nellie figured she could always slide the envelope under the apartment door. In fact, she'd prefer it that way.

When they got to the landing, Peggy reached past her to knock. Nellie wasn't used to being the timid one, but then Peggy had nothing to lose here. At first it seemed no one would answer, but after Peggy's second knock, the door opened.

Jay's mom, Mrs. Hostetler, a small woman with short, brown hair, raised her eyebrows. "Nellie? Peggy?"

"Hi," Nellie said, shifting her weight. "I stopped to drop something off for Jay and they told me to try up here."

"He's making a delivery for the Superette," Mrs. Hostetler said. "But I'll give it to him." She held out her hand.

As Nellie passed her the envelope, Mrs. Hostetler gave her a sad smile. "I'd ask you in, but I'm leaving for work. I clean the rest rooms downstairs before the Saturday night rush and I don't want to be late. We can't both get fired."

16

A Find at the Auction

That evening Nellie lay back on Peggy's bed and groaned. "I got him *fired*, Peg. He was broke before, and now he doesn't even have a job."

Peggy had her toes hooked under her dresser and was puffing her way through sit-ups. She stopped a moment and panted, then said, "Crime doesn't pay. It was his own fault for stealing."

"If he really did."

"Oh, Nellie, quit it. You thought about all this before you called the police. Now it's done, so forget it."

Peggy got up and began brushing her curls. "He did it to himself. It's like they say, 'If you won't do the time, don't do the crime.' "

"I guess." Nellie slid under the covers. "Do you want to go to the auction with me tomorrow afternoon?"

"Sounds like fun. Maybe I'll find old books."

"Ugh. How can you stand to touch those dirty things?"

"They kill my allergies," Peggy admitted, "but I can't help it—I just love them."

"I'm just hoping I'll find some good stuff—cheap—for Christmas presents. There probably won't be anything for Danny, though. And Aunt Paula's taking me, so I can't really get her anything without her knowing."

After Peggy shut off the light, Nellie's eyes stared at the faint outline of the closet door. There probably wasn't any point getting anything for Rick, either.

She drew a breath around the pain in her chest. Girls like Nellie didn't exactly attract a ton of boys to begin with. Why did she ever open her big, stupid mouth about Jay?

Thinking about Rick's big warm smile and the way he used to hold her hand was like a burning place in her heart. She turned on her side; a hot tear slid over her cheek.

*　*　*

Peggy leaned close enough so Nellie could hear her mutter, "Who's ever going to buy this junk?" She flipped through the cardboard box, picking up a battered watch, an ashtray, and two keys.

Nellie looked down the length of the table. "To tell the truth, I think a lot of it's Chlorine's." She grinned and pointed to a plaque featuring two pink-breasted turtledoves on a lime-green branch. "I even remember seeing this."

Peggy shuddered. "Old books are one thing. But used hairbrushes. Rusty tools. Ugh."

Nellie shrugged. "There's good stuff mixed in. That's the way these things work. You never know what you'll find."

"Spiders. A case of the plague."

"Look here," Nellie said. "This old cash register must be solid brass. It's an antique."

"So are these 'Paul Revere & the Raiders' CD's."

"Those aren't CD's. They're called eight-track tapes. And look at the record albums. Honestly, people collect them."

"Well, I don't see anything I'd want," Peggy said. "Except maybe a burger and some fries." She eyed the lunch counter and took a deep breath of the scorched meat aroma.

"Okay. Just a sec. Let me look through this stuff real quick."

The auction occupied the 4-H exhibit building at the County Fairgrounds. It seemed odd, coming here when everything was dusted with snow and deserted, except for the auction barn. Inside, the chatter of voices and squeak of folding chairs echoed off the concrete floor.

Tables along one side of the room held sales items. Bidders sat on the other side, eating chips and drinking coffee and pop as they craned their necks to see what items were coming up.

As the auction was about to get underway,

Nellie finally saw something she wanted—a set of Petunia Pig glasses for Mom. "Come on; let's grab those seats near the back."

"Can't we get our food?" Peggy asked. She already had her money out.

Nellie shot another look at the people filing into chairs. "Look." She pulled out a couple bills and gave them to Peggy. "Why don't I hold the seats and you can bring me a root beer and some fries?"

As she claimed her seat, Nellie threw her jacket over the one beside it to hold a spot for Peggy. She could see Aunt Paula all the way across the room, sipping from a paper cup with a teabag tag hanging over the side.

Nellie arranged herself so she'd be ready to bid. She loved the excitement of auctions.

The auctioneer, who looked like Santa Claus in a ponytail and cowboy hat, was gesturing at the first item. The runner, a skinny black guy in jeans, held an old phonograph up for the crowd as the bidding began.

Peggy had been right about the junk. By the time she came back, balancing a full cardboard tray of food, Nellie had sat through the sale of boxes of musty clothing, ancient Christmas decorations, and an exercise bike that must have been thirty years old.

Nellie's root beer sloshed as Peggy passed it over. She set it on her knee while she wiped up sticky droplets with a tissue, then took her greasy box of fries.

"Was your stuff up yet?" Peggy asked.

Nellie shook her head as the auctioneer tried to raise the bid on a set of old Boy Scout booklets and supplies. "Twenty, twenty-five. Will you give me twenty-five? How about twenty-one? Would that help you any?"

More items came and went, including a rusty lawn mower. "Fella brought it in said it worked real good," the auctioneer told them as the runner gave a mighty tug on the starter cord.

"Oh, well." The auctioneer shrugged at the silence.

Finally a runner carried out the box of Petunia Pig glasses. She set it on the table and held up a glass.

"Here's a whole set of pig glasses—that's whatzername. Eight glasses. And some other good stuff in here, too."

The runner waved measuring spoons with one hand and a can of motor oil with the other.

"Anyone know what this windup thing is?" the auctioneer asked.

He only got a few head shakes from the crowd.

"Well, it's a box of miscellaneous. Here we go. This whole box for one money. Who'll give a dollar for it?"

Nobody seemed excited. Nellie beat out a bored-looking woman for $1.50. She was now the proud owner of eight pig glasses and a lot of other stuff she hadn't even seen yet.

By the time she'd paid the clerk and claimed her box of treasures, Aunt Paula was bidding on braided rag rugs. Peggy helped Nellie drag the box to their seats and Nellie sifted through it.

"Oh, look. Here's an old-fashioned bottle-opener. Maybe I can give this to Dad. It looks antique-y."

Suddenly, her hands stopped sorting. There was a little cushion, printed with sprigs of violets, that fit inside the palm of her hand. It smelled sweet, like an old lady's flower garden. Beside it lay an embroidered hankie with lace around the edges.

Nellie sat with the sachet in one hand and the hankie in the other. Her brain was racing and her heart pounded.

"Smell this," she commanded, shoving the sachet under Peggy's nose. "What does this smell like?"

She shrugged. "I don't know. Bubblebath?"

"Is it lavender?"

"How should I know?"

Nellie fidgeted. "It is. I know it is. And see this?" She waved the hankie.

"What?" Peggy stopped it in mid-wave.

"See the initial embroidered in the corner? It's an 'E.' And the lady said she was sending a lavender sachet and a nice hankie to Aunt Bet."

"Who said?"

Nellie took a breath and tried to slow down. "Okay. When the mail got stolen at the Lucky Clover, there was a lady who said she was sending stuff to her aunt. I think this is it." She waved them at Peggy again. "It's part of the loot."

"Oh, Nell. Everybody has stuff like that."

"Not really. For one thing, it's lavender."

"Maybe."

"Well, if it is. Here they are, right together. And the initial on the hankie matches."

" 'Bet' doesn't start with an E, Nellie. I know you're not a great speller, but—"

"No, I know Bet doesn't start with an E, but who's named Bet, anyway? I'll *bet*," she giggled, "that Bet's short for Elizabeth. Which *does* begin with an E."

Peggy looked unconvinced.

"Peggy! I know—I just know—this is part of the loot. This means Rick and Mom were right. Jay didn't do it after all."

Peggy picked up a dancing-girl lamp. "If you're right, Nell, it means something else. It means Chlorine did it."

Nellie recognized that lamp, too. "Oh, shoot. Now what do I do?"

Peggy set it back in the box. "How about nothing? What's the matter with just staying out of it? You suspect Jay and report him, and then you feel all horrible about causing him trouble. Now you suspect Chlorine. What makes you think you're right this time?"

"It all fits, Peg. She needs a lot of money for food and electricity and taking care of all those animals. And she's bored with her life and looking for excitement."

"Nellie." Peggy gave her a look of strained patience. "She's an old lady and she doesn't drive.

How do you think she got down to the Lucky Clover to rob mailboxes—have the senior citizen's van service drop her off?"

"You saw her, Peggy. She looks like she could climb Mt. Everest. There's no reason she couldn't walk as far as the Lucky Clover. Besides, maybe she's not even in this alone."

"Maybe Jay's her accomplice," Peggy suggested with a snort.

"Oh, Peggy, the weird thing is, I don't want to get her in trouble, either. I like her—kind of. But I just know this proves Jay's innocent." She waved the hankie at Peggy. "After what I did to him, how can I not try to clear his name?"

"Nellie, the evidence is what it is. You just reported it. I don't see where you have any duty to prove anything. Forget about it. It's none of your business, anyway."

"If I get Jay out of trouble, maybe Rick will forgive me," Nellie mumbled. She wondered uncomfortably if she'd be willing to blame anybody for stealing that mail, just as long as it put things back the way they were with Rick.

17

Equal Opportunities in Crime

It was dark when Aunt Paula dropped Nellie off at the house. Behind its yellow-lit windows, she could hear Lady barking.

Dooley, Aunt Paula's big, shaggy mutt, crawled halfway over the seat to sniff the air through Nellie's open door. He barked back.

"I'll try to sneak my package into the back of the car after church on Sunday," Nellie said. "Then I can figure out how to get it up to my room from there."

"No rush," Aunt Paula said. "It's a joy just having that lamp in my home for a while." She grinned.

"Yeah," Nellie agreed. "It's just the touch of elegance your living room needs." She climbed out and paused, holding the door. "Thanks again."

"My pleasure," Paula said over Dooley's barks.

Nellie picked her way across icy spots on the flagstones leading to the porch. She'd brought home the sachet and the hankie so she could talk to Mom and Dad about them. She'd also grabbed a ceramic wall plaque of fruit, painted in explosive red and poisonous yellow-and-green. She figured she had to have something to show for her day at the auction.

"Nell, where's Paula?" Mom looked up from setting the kitchen table.

"She was expecting a phone call," Nellie said, hanging up her coat. "I think it's love."

"Could be." Mom smiled. "What did you buy?"

Nellie held up the plaque. "For the kitchen. I know it's kind of loud, but it reminded me a little of the one Grandma has on her wall."

Lady sniffed, analyzing her feet and legs. Then she wagged and pushed her muzzle into Nellie's hand, apparently having identified her friend Dooley's scent.

"That's nice, Nellie." Mom poked a fork into a pan of potatoes on the cookstove. "Guess these are ready now, if you want to call Dad and Danny."

"Sure." Nellie knew Mom would have said anything was nice, rather than hurt Nellie's feelings. Even if she'd brought home the dancing girl lamp, it would have become the focal point of the living room.

Dad was setting up his toy train layout in front of the tree, while Danny chewed on the flap of a cardboard box. "Come and get it," Nellie said. "I have something I need to talk to you and Mom about."

"Hi, Nell." Dad smiled over his shoulder, not budging as he fiddled with something underneath a tiny caboose. "Be right there."

But when Nellie finally had everyone together around the table, she toyed with a forkful of bean loaf. She wasn't sure how to tell about the hankie and sachet. She wanted some help, yet she didn't want to confess to turning Jay in to the police. Maybe she wouldn't need to get into that.

Finally, she just plunged right in. "I need some advice," she said, shoving a big brave forkful of bean loaf into her mouth. It wasn't her favorite of Mom's endless array of vegetarian dinners. Danny's cardboard box couldn't have been much drier.

"About what?" Mom asked.

Nellie explained about finding the hankie and sachet. She was careful to tell only enough, without letting on that she'd also bought their Christmas presents.

"I think it's part of the mailbox loot," she concluded, briefly telling about the gifts for Aunt Bet.

"Oh, honey, I don't know," Mom said. "That seems awfully thin." All the same, Nellie saw a glimmer of interest in her eyes.

"Let's see them," Dad said, and Nellie jumped up, eager to escape her bean loaf.

She carried the evidence back to the table, still wrapped in a tissue, then opened the package. "I don't think cloth will hold a fingerprint," she said, "Besides, I was already holding it before I realized it could be important. But maybe the sachet has a print on it."

Dad examined the hankie, then lifted the sachet by a corner. "Nell, they look pretty generic to me."

"What?"

"They're both pretty common, ordinary items."

"Smell it," Nellie urged. "Does it smell like lavender?"

He passed it under his nose, then handed it to Mom. "I don't know. Can you tell?"

Mom nodded. "Yes, I'd say that's lavender."

"That's what the lady said was in the envelope she was mailing," Nellie said eagerly. "And the hankie—"

"Honey," Mom said gently, "they sell these by the hundreds."

"But it has an initial on it."

Mom smiled and shrugged. "I guess the woman could at least say if it looks like what she lost."

"Maybe it will be enough to get Jay off the hook," Nellie said.

"I wish it would." Mom sighed. "But they found ripped-open envelopes in his car that can be positively identified. It looks pretty bad for him, Nellie."

Nellie swallowed, folding the tissue around her evidence. Mom reached over and squeezed her shoulder. "I'm so proud of you. It's wonderful how you're trying to help Jay. He needs all the friends he can get."

Nellie couldn't look up. This was the worst—having Mom praise her for trying to help. If she only knew the truth.

Dad helped himself to more bean loaf. "Your supper's getting cold. Why don't you eat?"

"I don't feel too good," she said, and it was actually the truth.

"Will they be able to tell at the auction where a couple little things like that came from?" he asked.

Nellie's lips tightened. That was the next problem. "Well—they were in one of the boxes of Chlorine's stuff."

Mom and Dad looked at each other. "Oh, now, Nellie," Dad began.

"I know; I know. But her initial isn't E," Nellie said stubbornly.

Dad shook his head. "I knew a guy named Gus who wore secondhand coveralls to work. One day his pocket would say 'Manuel,' and the next day he was 'Ken.' "

"I just can't imagine she'd be out stealing mail," Mom said. "And I don't want to make trouble for an innocent old woman."

"But there could be other reasons why the stuff ended up in that box," Nellie said. "And we'll never know. It's evidence. Shouldn't Jay at least get a chance to clear himself here? Chlorine can always tell her side of things, too."

Again Mom sighed and rubbed her head.

"How do we get in the middle of these things?"

"Well, for what it's worth, I think Jay's entitled to the benefit of any evidence that tends to clear him," Dad said, lifting Danny from his seat as he began to fuss.

"I suppose you're right," Mom said. "Maybe we'll never have to implicate Chlorine, anyway. The police may not take this seriously, you know."

A phone call quickly proved her right. When Dad finally made the call, he soon got the message that the police weren't looking for any help from amateur detectives.

"They wouldn't even listen," he said, shaking his head. "As a citizen, I must say I resent it. The officer on duty was very patronizing: 'Old ladies do use sachets, sir, and hankies, too. There's nothing that distinctive about what you're describing.' "

Nellie listened in disbelief. It had never occurred to her that anyone wouldn't take her dad seriously—especially people who take anonymous tips from kids. "Wouldn't they at least try showing it to the lady who was mailing that stuff?"

"Oh, they'll take it, but they didn't promise to do anything at all with it. In fact, he said that even if these were the missing items, they could simply have been blown away and picked up by an innocent passerby."

"I think we have to recognize, too, that those crumpled envelopes in Jay's car are still a big problem," Mom said. "Even I wonder how he ended up with them."

"I have a theory on that," Nellie said. "I think Chlorine could have planted them on him when he was making his grocery delivery."

"But how?" Dad asked. "He probably just brought the stuff to the door and she paid him and he left."

"But we don't know," Nellie insisted. "She's no weakling. She probably only gets deliveries because she doesn't drive. Maybe she helped carry bags in from the car."

"I think you're stretching," Mom said. "Besides, that's awfully fast work for an eighty-year-old amateur criminal—to walk a mile each way and steal mail before breakfast, then plant the evidence on someone the same morning."

"Well, maybe," Nellie said darkly, "she isn't an amateur."

18

More Trouble for Jay

The next morning Nellie lingered outside the door to their Sunday school room. She'd made Mom and Dad—who usually ran at least five minutes late—hurry to get there early.

She really wanted to catch Rick before he went in, to explain and apologize and try to make things right between them. It was hard, though, lurking in the hallway and looking up each time someone came downstairs. It was even harder to answer the questioning looks with "I'm waiting for somebody."

At last she heard Rick's familiar step and looked up into his startled dark eyes. Her stomach twisted into a hard knot.

"Rick—" She stepped from among the coats hanging along the wall.

"Hey, Nellie." He came up to her uneasily.

"Look," they both said at once, then grinned sheepishly.

"Look," Rick repeated. "Nellie, I'm sorry. I've been a real jerk and wasn't fair to you. I wish things were different, but you were only doing what you thought was right. I can't stand it like this."

"Me neither. Oh, Rick, I was so stupid not to at least talk to Mom about things. And honestly, I never wanted to make trouble for Jay. I'm so sorry." She looked down to blink away sudden tears.

"Hey, it's okay." Rick grabbed Nellie's shoulders and pulled her into a hug. "Let's not fight anymore."

A step on the stairway made them move awkwardly apart. Their teacher, Miss Snyder, smiled when she saw them. "Good morning."

She opened the door and Nellie moved to follow her, leaning just close enough to whisper to Rick, "Talk to you after class."

Later, in the ten minutes between Sunday school and church, Nellie, Rick, and Peggy stayed in their classroom and talked. Nellie explained what had turned up among Chlorine's auction treasures.

In seconds, Rick's face lit with excitement and as quickly crumpled. "Oh, Nellie, it would be great to prove Jay didn't steal that mail. But Chlorine! You can't honestly believe that."

Seeing Nellie's expression, he added, "Okay. You do believe it. But nobody else will."

"Why?" Nellie demanded. "Are you prejudiced against old people? They can be crooks, too, you know."

"Boy, there's some great news for senior citizens," Rick snorted. "No age discrimination for illegal activities."

He held up one arm as she tried to swat him. "Take it easy. I didn't mean people won't believe it because she's old. It's because she's Chlorine. It's just not her style."

"You don't know that," Nellie argued, watching his face for signs she was making him mad again. "Just think about it." Quickly, she ran through all the reasons Chlorine had for stealing mail.

"You know," Rick said, "the more you say that stuff, the more sense it makes."

Rick ran a hand through his hair. "And that should tell you something. Look, Nellie, I guess I just hate to think she did it—let alone frame Jay for it."

"I know," Nellie said. "I do, too. But we can't always expect the truth to be the way we'd like it to be."

"I guess." Rick's voice was reluctant.

"Look," Nellie said. "Just say she did do it, okay? And say we didn't want to get her in trouble, so we kept our mouths shut. But what if Jay got sent to jail for it? Is that what you want?"

"Well, no. Of course not. But what are you going to do about it, anyway? The cops already don't believe you."

"I've been thinking about that," Nellie told him. "The only thing we *can* do is hope she still has some evidence around the house."

Rick raised his eyebrows.

"Well, I did promise Peg and I would go back there and help out some more. We can all go, and really keep our eyes open."

Next Saturday was a perfect day for going to Chlorine's—one of those winter days when the sun's so bright you have to squint and the air feels like spring. Nellie felt as if anything could happen.

She walked to Chlorine's, kicking at melting lumps of snow with her boots. The woods were full of light, and the few brown leaves that clung to the trees twisted and spun like dancers in the breeze.

Nellie breathed faster, passing the place where she'd seen the watcher among the trees. The woods seemed so different today, but automatically her eyes searched the ground for prints. Nothing but deer and rabbits.

She scanned the trees. Everything looked normal, and yet she wondered.

What was that shape among the cluster of dark trunks and hemlocks? She stopped, ears straining, holding her breath, and stared. *A crooked tree.*

She studied a curve here, an angle there. *It must be a crooked tree*, she told herself. It didn't move, and the only sound was an occasional soft rustle like the passage of a small animal.

Nellie began walking again, realizing her heart was beating just a little faster. A few more steps—and she whirled around.

Now she couldn't see that gnarled tree. Maybe from this angle it just blended in.

She hurried on.

As Nellie neared Chlorine's driveway, she could see Rick along the road ahead. His head was down despite the dazzling sunshine, and he shuffled his feet.

She'd opened her mouth to yell, "Hey, Rick!" But something about the way he was walking made her stop in her tracks and close her mouth.

Rick's hands were jammed in his jacket pockets and his shoulders hunched into his turned-up collar. He looked like he was cold, or maybe just plain miserable.

As she came closer, Nellie cleared her throat. "Hey, Rick!"

He raised his head, an overcast look darkening his face. "Hi."

When they were only a few feet apart, they stopped. "It happened again."

"What?" Nellie crinkled her forehead.

"Another mail robbery." Rick's lips pressed together in a frustrated line. "Jay got called in again."

19

The Search Continues

Nellie and Rick stood, staring at each other by the foot of the driveway. Chlorine's dog pack set up a wild barking from the trampled mud and snow of the yard. Nellie heard them dimly, like a ringing in her ears.

"Did they arrest him?"

Rick shook his head. "I don't think they have enough evidence. They were just checking his whereabouts."

"Well, at least—" Nellie started.

Rick shook his head. "They didn't arrest him yet. But this will probably be all over town anyway. I'm just afraid he won't be able to get another job at all. No high school diploma, an arrest record—and right before Christmas, too."

The sound of a car made them turn. Mrs. Penwick stopped a few feet away and let Peggy out. "Call me when you're done. Otherwise, I'll stop on the way back—all right?"

Mrs. Penwick smiled and waved as she crept on past them. Nellie raised her eyebrows questioningly at Peggy.

"She said she might as well sit and talk to your mom instead of driving all the way home and back again." Peggy seemed to notice Rick's expression. "What's up?"

He explained, then added, "Let's just get in there and get done. It's why we're here."

"Maybe we'll find something," Nellie said encouragingly.

"Well, she didn't do this one." Rick pointed at the driveway.

Nellie's heart flopped. "No fresh tracks. But maybe she went another way."

"Sure, hopping down the Sasquatch trail."

"Well, maybe, Rick," Peggy defended her. "If she didn't want to be seen along the road. I'll bet there are tons of paths through the woods."

He considered as they slogged their way up the driveway. "There sure used to be when Fred and I hiked up this way. Before Chlorine moved in, and Fred had his accident. But it's been a couple years and trails disappear pretty fast."

"Not if somebody still uses them." Nellie grabbed his arm as Chlorine came out on her porch. "Did they lead back to the road somewhere farther down?" she hissed.

Rick nodded. "Couple places."

"Too bad nobody thought to check there for tracks the last time," Peggy said.

"Where was this one?" Nellie asked, trying

hard to keep her voice down.

"I don't know," Rick admitted. "It might not even be walking distance for her."

"Darlings!" Chlorine stood ready to welcome them, the dogs hanging back at a respectful distance.

"Hi, Miss LaFontayne." Nellie noticed she was birdwoman again. One swooping feather had gotten bent, and it hung down over one eye to lend an air of mystery.

"Do come in, my good Samaritans. Forgive the chill. I try to keep the heat low."

Nellie grinned, watching Rick take in the living room for the first time. As his eye traveled all the way around the room, from the Hawaiian sunset painted on black velvet to a fringed footstool that looked like an especially ugly lapdog, he forgot to close his mouth.

Before she got all the way inside, Peggy sneezed enormously.

"God bless you, dear child!" Chlorine looked around in bewilderment. "Now where did I leave that box of tissues?"

"It's okay, ma'am. I've got my own." Peggy dug a tissue from her coat pocket and had it clamped to her nose before the next big sneeze.

"Oh, dear. I do believe you're catching a cold. Perhaps I should turn up the heat, after all."

"No." Peggy shook her head as she wiped. "It's just allergies. But maybe I'd better stay outside. Is there anything I can do out there?"

"Oh, my, yes. I just have work *everywhere*.

Even that barn, well—" The red feathers fluttered as Chlorine waved her arms. "You children are so good to offer your help. Why don't you all just come through here?"

Feeling like a duckling waddling after its huge, red mother, Nellie followed the others through the kitchen to the back porch. Grocery bags stuffed with old newspapers and other scrap paper stood in piles as high as her shoulder.

Chlorine pointed over it to a rusting barrel in the center of the backyard. "That's my burn barrel. I just never seem to get around to carting all this over there."

"Do you want all this burned?" Rick asked.

"Well . . ." Chlorine considered. "Enough to fill the barrel for now."

"We all might as well help with this first," Nellie said. "We'll check with you when we get it taken care of."

"Excellent, excellent." Chlorine beamed. "I'll be sure to have some nice, hot tea ready to warm you up."

Nellie hid a grimace as she turned to pick up a grocery bag. She was in no hurry to bleach her tonsils with that stuff again.

"This is perfect," she whispered as the door closed. "Looks like all the scrap paper in the house. All we have to do is pull it out of the bags when we fill the barrel—and keep our eyes open."

"She can see us out the back window," Rick reminded. "So we can't be too obvious."

"No problem." Nellie eased down the two rickety steps to the yard. "Smooth is my middle name."

The burn barrel sat in an open space several feet from the back fence. Nellie set her bag beside it and, turning her back to the house, pulled out a handful of paper.

She fanned it out so she could see at a glance what she had. Newspapers. Junk mail. She threw it in the barrel with one hand while the other grabbed a second wad of paper.

Rick and Peggy dropped bags on either side of her and began pulling out stuff. "We'll never get through all this," Peggy muttered.

"Enough of it," Nellie assured her. "All we have to do is look at the dates on the papers on top, and pick bags that have stuff from after the robbery."

Peggy looked doubtful and Rick shrugged.

By cramming the papers down as they stuffed them in the barrel, they were able to clear nearly half the porch of bags. The top of the barrel already sprouted with tufts of paper as Nellie scanned her last handful.

"Hey!" She froze, staring at a card-sized envelope in her hand.

"What is it?" Peggy and Rick crowded around her before all three glanced nervously at the back windows. No sign of Chlorine. They looked down again.

"See," Nellie said. "It's not addressed to her. It says 'Maggie Bugnickel.' "

"So she does have someone else's mail," Peggy said. "But I wonder where the rest of it is."

"This is probably just one she missed when she planted that stuff on Jay." Nellie glanced at the house again, then back at the envelope. "No box number," she mumbled. "Just R.D. 2, Begg City."

"Quick, hide it!" Peggy whispered. "The door's opening."

20

Terror in the Barn

If Chlorine had seen what they were up to, she hid it well. She stood with her hands on her hips and admired the porch. "My, you children work fast. And doesn't this porch look nice? Why, we'll soon be ready for the magazine photographers."

"Magazine?" Peggy asked.

Chlorine laughed "You never know. After all, that Sasquatch incident did get a lot of attention."

Nellie raised a furtive eyebrow at Rick, but he didn't seem to notice.

"Won't you come in for a nice cup of tea now?"

Nellie was about to excuse herself from the tea party when she realized this would be her chance to snoop around the inside. "Sure, thanks."

As she and Rick headed for the steps, she could feel the scrape of the envelope in her pocket. She pushed down her guilty feelings about snooping, remembering what she'd already found.

"I'll just stay out here," Peggy said. "Allergies. Maybe I could sweep your porch."

But as she said it, the dog pack came around the corner, maybe attracted by Chlorine's voice. Behind them trotted the goat.

"Oh, mercy! How'd they get loose?" Chlorine shook her head and beamed like an affectionate mother at her flock of sweet but naughty children. "I thought I had them penned in the front yard."

Peggy crossed the yard and was on the porch in five jumps. The animals followed her, grinning as if they enjoyed the chase.

"Stay!" Chlorine commanded, standing at the edge of the porch like a traffic cop.

The dogs stopped at the foot of the steps, ducking their heads with a look of foolish apology. The goat, however, came right on up.

"Augustus!" Chlorine bellowed as the goat pushed right past her, shaking his long horns.

He nibbled at the hem of Peggy's jacket with his long upper lip and she pulled away.

"Ma-aa," he complained.

"Well, you might as well come on in," Chlorine told them, pushing open the back door. "I'll get you that tea, then deal with these miscreants." She smiled at Augustus, who was the first one to push through the door.

Looking back at the dogs waiting at the foot

of the steps, Peggy followed the goat. The kitchen table was set with a colorful array of cups and saucers—blue violets, orange and green stripes, yellow roses. A horrible smell drifted from the white teapot, which was shaped like a cat with its uplifted paw for a spout.

"Here." Chlorine began lifting papers from the chairs. "Sit, sit."

She placed a plate of grayish lumps on the table. At first Nellie thought they were dried clumps of mud. Then she decided they must be oatmeal cookies.

As Chlorine turned to pull a sugar bowl from the cupboard, Gus the goat strolled to the table and began eating cookies. "Hey!" she said softly, turning back, and pushed his nose away from the plate.

"You go ahead and enjoy your tea," she said. She set down the sugar and shoved the cookies to the center of the table. "I'm going to pen these good-for-nothings back up."

Rick slid into the empty chair. As soon as the front door clicked, he leaned in, holding one hand over his nose and mouth. "That goat smells awful."

"It's not the goat," Nellie told him. "Quick —before she gets back." She jumped up and poured tea in each cup. "Swish it around and dump most of it in the sink."

"What is this stuff?" Rick asked.

Nellie shrugged, emptying the pot down the drain. "Hurry up."

When the pot and cups held only a few drops, Nellie looked around the room. "We don't have much time. Why don't we each take a room?"

"And do what?" Peggy frowned.

"Check the wastebaskets for more envelopes or anything like that. And try to notice if it looks like she's suddenly spending money."

"On what?" Rick asked. "It doesn't look like she ever spends money."

"That's just because you were never in here before," Nellie said. "Peggy or I might see a difference. Now let's go."

Without giving them a chance to argue, Nellie hurried into the bedroom. Hands shaking, she pawed through the overflowing wastebasket. The light was dim, so she had to squint. Nothing but trash.

Her eyes darted around the room at the threadbare bedspread, chipped dresser, and frayed pink throw rug. Rick was right. It did look like Chlorine hadn't spent a nickel in the last ten years.

The squawk of the front door made Nellie jump. Almost running for the kitchen, she tried to erase the guilty feelings that must be showing on her face.

Peggy was sneezing at the kitchen table and Rick was eating one of the cookies the goat had missed. Nellie shook her head. Boys' appetites were amazing.

Chlorine burst red-cheeked into the room through the other doorway. She didn't seem to notice the quick look that passed between Nellie and her friends, or the slight shake of the head that meant none of their searches had been successful.

"That should hold those pesky critters awhile," Chlorine said with satisfaction. "More tea?"

"No thanks," Nellie quickly replied. "We came to work, so we'd better get back to it."

"How about the barn, ma'am?" Rick asked. "You said something earlier."

"Oh, my, yes. The previous owner used it for storage—all kinds of rubble. And he just left it all. I keep meaning to clear it out. Then Augustus and the dogs would have a place of their own. But I just never seem to have the time."

She looked at Peggy, who was blowing her nose. "But then I thought how dusty it is in there for anyone with allergies."

"Well, Nellie and I aren't allergic," Rick told her. "We could at least get started in there today."

"I can sweep the porch now," Peggy said.

"Well, all right." Chlorine took a broom from behind the back door. "And you other kids just pile the rubble from the barn right alongside so I can get it hauled away. Anything worth saving—and I doubt there's much—you just stick it in the front stall."

As they tramped outside, Nellie leaned near Peggy and whispered, "Check the rest of the bags."

Chlorine led Nellie and Rick across the back-yard toward the barn. Passing the corner of the house, Nellie stopped, glimpsing the road. "Hey, it's—" She cast through her brain for the name of the kid in the blue and red parka.

Rick and Chlorine looked up at once. "Mike!" Rick said.

"Oh, it's my little friend!" Chlorine waved and smiled. "Back here, Mike! Don't let the animals out."

In a moment Mike was lifting the bent piece of wire that served as Chlorine's gate latch. "Hi," Rick and Nellie told him.

He didn't answer but turned to Chlorine. "Hi, Grandma. What's the matter?" His eyes were troubled as he darted a quick look at Nellie and Rick.

"Well, hi, Mike. These are my friends, Nellie and Rick. And Peggy," she added, pointing. "They've just come to help me get caught up with some of this work around the place."

"Hi, Mike," Rick said.

Mike gave him a look only slightly warmer than a glare. "I can help you," he told her. "You don't need somebody else."

She patted his shoulder. "Now, Mike, just the barn alone is a huge job. It's too big for one person. You're sweet to offer, but it'll go a lot better with all of you."

"But Grandma!" Mike looked desperate as he planted his stocky body between them and the barn. "I want to do it myself. Can't I, please?"

134

Chlorine studied his anxious dark eyes and flushed cheeks. "Oh, now, Mike. Don't be silly."

She smiled. "You know what's important to me, so you can be in charge. You help them separate out anything worth saving. But as Great-Aunt Sadie used to say, 'Many hands make light work.'"

"We just want to help," Rick said gently. "You tell us what to do."

Even so, Chlorine almost had to lift him out of the way, so she could pass. At once he stepped back into Nellie and Rick's path, walking slowly backward in front of them.

"It's a real mess in there," he warned. "Grandma never used it. The mice built nests and there are spiders all over the place." He looked at Nellie as if he expected her to run the other way.

Having had mice as pets when she was little, and crying at the end each time she'd read *Charlotte's Web*, Nellie just smiled. "Sounds like it does need a cleaning."

"It's dusty and moldy, too. And dark."

"I guess we'll have to wash up afterward," Nellie said.

"And we'll open the doors and windows for light," Rick told him.

Chlorine turned the wooden door latch with a scrape. Mike jumped. "Here's the nasty old rat's nest," she chuckled. "I'll see you when you're through."

When Chlorine got out of earshot, Nellie grabbed Mike's jacket sleeve. "Hey, Mike, it's okay. I understand how you feel. The barn's—like private to you. It's your special place. Don't worry. We'll mind our business and do what you say."

He didn't answer. He just pulled away and stepped toward the door, but Nellie slipped in ahead of him.

As she stepped over the threshold, the smell of must and damp crept up her nose. The air was thick with dust and moldy hay and mouse nests.

She shuffled her feet, eyes adjusting to blackness. Somewhere overhead, something scurried on quick small feet. Loose dirt rained onto her hair and shoulders.

On the left, cobweb-draped stanchions stood where someone had once milked cows. Black holes of open stall doors gaped on the right.

Another step in. And another. Nellie's eyes adapted and she could see the hard, grayed remains of a halter hanging from a nail near the last stall. Nellie looked down.

Instantly, she recoiled, scrambling backward into Rick as she screamed in horror.

21

The Barn's Secret

Rick's heart pounded against her shoulder. "Nellie, what is it?"

"It's horrible," Nellie gasped, fighting down a shudder that shook her whole body.

"What?" He tried to look around her. "Where?"

"There on the floor by the stall door," Nellie told him, shuddering again.

She turned around to point, slowly so Rick would keep his arm around her. All the same, her tense body wanted to run.

Mike already had. He was standing back outside, peering through the door.

She and Rick stared at the floor. Rick laughed, but it sounded shaky.

"Well, you're right. It *is* hideous."

Nellie took a gulp of stale air. She knew it was harmless, but the mummified-looking cat was the creepiest thing she'd ever seen.

How long had it been dead? Probably at least since summer, when the baking heat had shriveled it into a leathery museum piece.

Mike popped up between them and the mummy, laughing. "Is that all that's bothering you? I told you guys it was awful in here. You better just let me handle it."

Nellie stood straighter and concentrated on not shaking. "It just startled me. That's all."

Mike grinned. "There's dead birds, too."

"Well, then I guess we need to start cleaning," Rick said matter-of-factly.

"How about starting with that front stall then? There's not much in it but old hay."

Nellie looked back. The front stall stood right next to the open door, where it was a little brighter and a fresh breeze moved the stale air. Though she felt tempted, she couldn't help wondering why Mike suggested it.

Was he being nice? Or did he just want to make it clear that he was in charge here?

"Is Chlorine really your grandmother?" Nellie asked.

Even in the dimness, she could see Mike's face redden. He looked away; at first, she thought he wouldn't answer. "No. I just call her that."

"Come on, Nellie. We'd better get going. At least we can get that stall cleaned out before we have to leave," Rick said.

Still, Nellie hesitated. There were two more stalls past the cat. Now that her eyes had adjusted and she was over her fright, she wanted to look through the rest of the barn.

While Rick turned toward the first stall, Nellie narrowed her gaze on Mike. He stood in the aisle, legs apart as if to block her.

Behind him, dust and hay fragments filtered down through the quiet air, spiraling against a curtain of shadows. Was he trying to hide something?

Nellie stepped closer, pretending interest in the former cat. "I guess Chlorine's like a special friend, huh?" She spoke casually, not looking at him.

"Yeah, I guess," Mike mumbled.

"I have some older friends like that too," Nellie told him. She slowly straightened back up, still looking down at the cat.

"Sometimes they seem to understand things better than anybody," she said, thinking of Mr. Spangler, who shared her love of old graveyards. "And I think they're—I don't know—*steadier* than kids my age."

She was close enough now. With one easy sidestep, Nellie slipped past Mike.

"Hey!"

"I'm just looking," she said calmly. "I won't touch anything."

A fierce tackle from behind almost knocked her down. "Hey, quit it!" Nellie yelled.

"What's going on?" Rick headed back the aisle.

Nellie struggled, trying to shake Mike loose from her waist. "Let go, kid. I'm just looking around."

"It's none of your business," Mike puffed, tightening his grip.

"Come on, Nellie. Forget it," Rick said, trying to pry loose Mike's arms.

Nellie broke free. "I just want to know what the big deal is. It's Chlorine's barn, and she let us in. All I want to do is look around." She looked back at Mike, who was teary-eyed as Rick held him with a restraining hand.

"I thought you came to help her!" Mike said. "But all you want is to snoop around. You don't even like Chlorine. I've heard you talking on the bus like she's a big joke." His voice shook with anger.

Nellie shuffled her feet. "I do like her, Mike. I like her a lot. And we did come to help her. Sometimes I guess I say stuff that sounds bad and —I'm sorry. I'm just being silly and kidding around."

"Come on, Nell," Rick repeated.

"Okay, sure. Just a minute." Nellie's eyes wandered to the shadowy back stalls.

Mike had been right about her, and she couldn't help feeling embarrassed. But she'd meant what she said about liking Chlorine, too. The problem was the detective in her, that curiosity that just wouldn't quit.

She turned and smiled at Mike to try to reassure him. "I promise not to pay attention to any of your secret stuff. I'm just taking a quick look around. We need to see how big a job we've got here, don't we?"

Mike stared at the floor. His shoulders sagged.

Nellie looked away, pushing down the guilt. Quickly, she walked to the next stall and peeked inside. Someone had stored a rusty wheelbarrow, picks and shovels with broken handles, and wooden boxes draped in dusty cobwebs. The boxes were stamped "Armour Star Corned Beef" and "Small Arms Ammunition—Winchester Repeating Co." It all looked undisturbed for the past twenty years.

Nellie knew she couldn't linger without arousing Mike's further suspicion. She moved on to the last stall. Beyond it, she could now see, was a narrow aisle leading to a back part of the barn. The building was bigger than she'd realized.

A glance into the stall revealed musty sacks of lime. How long ago had a farmer stored them there with plans to prepare his fields for planting? Dirty white powder lay like patchy snow where the bags had ruptured.

She turned the corner, feeling Mike grow tense at her back. The aisle closed around her, dark and stringy with dust-coated spiderwebs.

Nellie hurried through the narrow passageway. Her heart felt crowded in her chest.

The back section was wide and open, with low-sided wooden pens along the right. Probably for penning calves in the old days. Despite the windows along the opposite wall, she had to squint. The light filtering through the coating of grime was faint and gray.

Nellie let her eyes range over the row of calf-pen dividers. While they weren't much more than chest-high, murky shadows hid their contents.

At the farthest pen, her eyes rested. Something bulky stuck up above the low wall. Nellie swallowed.

Looking down at her feet, she could see the dust had been disturbed. Someone had been here before her, and recently.

She followed the smudgy trail to the last pen. Now she could see it.

Sticking out above the divider was a massive foot and leg that couldn't belong to any human. Nellie's heart pounded. First the cat. Now she'd found the carcass of a Sasquatch.

22

One Mystery Solved?

The back barn door squawked as Mike slipped through its narrow opening into the pasture. Nellie, skittish, whirled at the sound just as Rick came in through the passageway.

"Rick, look!" She clutched his arm, tugging him toward that last pen.

"Hey," Nellie said softly. She could see better now in the slim shaft of light from the open door.

What she'd thought was a foot was a shaggy bedroom slipper—or actually, two pieced together to make a single monster-sized one. They were the kind of slippers people got as a joke, with big furry toes and claws made of fuzzy tan felt.

Nellie let go of Rick's arm and walked up to the monster foot. She squished its toe. "It's stuffed."

"Yeah." Rick reached past her to thump the foot and poke his fingers inside the top opening. He examined the broom handle "leg." "This thing wouldn't fool an expert for a minute."

"Well, it fooled a lot of people," Nellie pointed out. "Even that researcher couldn't say for sure what it was."

"That's because the snow was mostly slush," Rick said. "You could hardly see anything but the size and general shape."

"I guess with clearer prints anyone could tell they were all made with just one right foot."

Rick nodded. "And there are other things, too. Like when an animal walks, you can see how the toes press down separately. This thing's just a block of wood—plop, plop, plop."

Nellie was quiet for a moment, imagining how someone might have created monster tracks good enough to fool an expert. Maybe he'd start in the woods at the fenceline, then plant the big foot and step in its tracks.

But how did someone get the foot back to the barn without messing up? She supposed you could walk backward in the same tracks, but you'd have to leap because of the big strides.

"You think Chlorine faked it?" she asked, unable to imagine her leaping backwards over the snow.

Rick shook his head. "I don't know. Why would she do something like that?"

Nellie shrugged. "Attention maybe. But I think it would be awful hard for her. And most older people—even if they're in good shape like she is—wouldn't want to risk falling by jumping all over the ice."

"You know who probably did it." Rick looked at the back door.

"I know." She lowered her voice. "That's why he was trying so hard to keep us out."

"The question's still why."

Nellie walked to the door and pushed it wider. Mike stood a few feet away, his face red and defiant but his shoulders drooping.

"Come on, Mike. Let's talk."

He didn't say anything, but a stubborn look settled across his face.

Rick appeared at Nellie's shoulder. "Hey, Mike. We don't want to cause you any trouble, but we've got to talk about this."

"I don't believe you." The words sounded choked. "You think Grandma's crazy. I heard you say so. All you want is to make fun of her."

Nellie looked at Rick. He was better with people than she was. Sometimes she felt she spent half her time sticking her foot in her mouth and the other half trying to pry it back out.

Rick met her eyes, then glanced back at Mike. "Look, Mike. Have you ever been kidding around and said something that really hurt someone's feelings? It's like Nellie said before. Sometimes we say stuff we don't really mean. We're sorry it sounded like that."

Nellie stepped a little closer. She reached for Mike's shoulder, but he jerked away. "Mike, I'm sorry," she said to his half-turned face. "We really don't want to get Chlorine in any trouble if we don't have to."

145

He didn't answer.

"Mike. We know it wasn't Chlorine, anyway. I'll bet she didn't even know, did she?"

This time, Mike did look around, and his eyes were scared. Nellie tensed in case he ran, but instead he squared his shoulders.

"She thought it was real," he mumbled. "Like the one she saw before. She *did*," he added, as if expecting her to laugh. "She did see a Big Foot. Grandma never lies."

Rick nodded. "I'm sure she really believes everything she told you," he said gently.

"She's not crazy, either," Mike said stubbornly, his cheeks growing redder. "If she thinks she saw something, she did."

"Okay," Rick said. "But Mike, why did you do this?"

Mike's eyes dropped; Nellie could hardly hear what he said. "To show you. To show everybody. You were so smart. I didn't want you making fun of her anymore."

Nellie felt her own cheeks steam with embarrassment. "We won't. Honest."

Rick tilted his head at him. "How'd you do this?"

Mike shrugged, not meeting their eyes. Despite his blushing cheeks, he looked almost smug. "I'm not telling."

"One thing we know," Nellie observed. "The dogs know him, so they probably never made a yip."

Mike looked up defiantly. "Am I in trouble?"

146

Nellie glanced back at Rick. They'd solved the Sasquatch mystery. They had to report it, didn't they?

Rick looked back at her with a shrug.

Should people be allowed to trick everybody and cause all kinds of trouble and just get away with it? But then, had it really been so much trouble?

Excitement was more like it. Nellie remembered the glow on Chlorine's face as she told the reporters her story. And Jeff—how thrilled he'd been. Even the neighbors had flocked to the farm for the big event.

Poor Mike. Looking at him, he seemed such a little kid, round-cheeked and scared. Trying to hide behind all that tough squawking. He hadn't done one thing that hurt anybody, not one thing out of meanness or just for kicks.

He'd filled that lonely place in his heart with Chlorine—and protected her with the fierce devotion of a faithful knight. Nellie sighed.

"No, Mike. Not from us. You're not in trouble."

Rick put a hand on his shoulder. "We won't tell anybody. But you can't do this anymore." His voice was stern. "It isn't right to fool people."

"I know," Mike mumbled, turning redder.

"I don't want to do it anymore. It made me feel creepy. Especially tricking Grandma."

"We believe you," Nellie said. "I get myself in trouble all the time."

"*All* the time," Rick echoed, grinning.

Nellie stuck her tongue out at him and continued. "I do stuff that seems right when I'm doing it, but it turns out wrong, then I feel awful."

For the first time, Mike met her eyes in a kind of recognition. He looked away again when Nellie smiled at him.

"I've gotta get home."

"Us, too," Rick said. "As soon as we do the front stall."

"You won't tell?" Mike asked again.

Rick shook his head. "Not unless you try something like this again."

When Mike's footsteps had died away, Nellie and Rick began forking moldy hay into the derelict wheelbarrow. Nellie tried not to breathe the musty smell.

"Good thing Peggy didn't come in here," she choked. "This is a real mold-spore mob scene."

"It's pretty bad," Rick agreed. "Come get some air while I dump this on her garden patch."

Nellie walked alongside as Rick shoved and lifted the stubborn wheelbarrow over the wet, uneven ground. She was glad to breathe the clean, damp air.

"Well," Nellie said, stretching, "if we were Nancy Drew—or the Hardy Boys," she quickly added, "we'd have solved the Mailbox Mystery today."

Rick grinned. "Hey, aren't you ever happy? We solved the Secret of the Sasquatch, you know."

"I know," Nellie grumped. "But the stolen mail's the real problem. If Nancy Drew, er, Joe Hardy, found a fake Sasquatch leg, it would all be part of the mail robbery somehow."

"Welcome to the real world," Rick said, dumping the hay. Using a booted foot, he spread it over the mucky ground.

Nellie helped kick the mulch in place. "Well, at least we found one stolen envelope. That's something, anyway."

It was late afternoon when Nellie and Rick walked back to the house. She stuck a hand in her pocket to touch the Maggie Bugnickel envelope, to assure herself it was real and she hadn't lost it.

The back porch looked much cleaner. Smoke was rising in a smudgy column from the trash barrel, and Peggy was nowhere in sight.

"Must be teatime." Nellie's mouth twisted in protest.

"Maybe she already finished it," Rick said hopefully.

Nellie shook her head gloomily. "Chlorine has a never-ending supply of that stuff." She sighed. "And you just dumped more fertilizer on her herb garden."

As they pushed open the back door into the kitchen, Nellie stopped in her tracks. How much cleaner the room was. The worn and cracked linoleum floor was actually damp.

Peggy sat at the table, a hefty, old-fashioned scrapbook open in front of her and one hand holding a tissue to her nose. She looked up when the door opened.

"Where's Chlorine?"

Peggy waved her tissue toward the front room. "Getting another scrapbook of her career."

Nellie looked over her shoulder at a yellowed newspaper photo of Chlorine in an Indian maiden costume. Despite many years' passage, Nellie didn't need a caption to recognize her. For one thing, she towered over the brave next to her. For another, that strong jaw was one of a kind.

"These really go back a way," Rick commented.

"They go further than this," Peggy told him. She flipped back the pages. "Look at this."

Nellie leaned in to see a small and faded clipping about some church's long-ago Christmas pageant. "See," Peggy hissed, jabbing a finger at one of the names.

Nellie squinted at the list of children. Someone named Gladys had snagged the role of Mary. Peggy was pointing at a name below hers.

"Herald of Joy," Nellie read. "Maggie Bugnickel."

23

Facing Jay

"It's her," Peggy whispered. "That's her real name. She changed it when she went to Hollywood."

Nellie's stomach lurched. "I should have known," she groaned. "Nobody's name is Chlorine."

Nellie didn't know whether to feel relieved or hopeless. Now she realized how much she liked Chlorine and didn't want her mixed up in something bad. But poor Jay!

"Someone from back home in West Virginia must still call her by her old name," Peggy said.

Nellie nodded. "All we've got now is that sachet and the hankie."

"And maybe the police are right," Rick said. "They could just be a coincidence."

A frenzy of barking came from the front yard. "Sounds like a car," Nellie said. "Maybe it's your mom," she told Peggy.

Peggy shook her head. "Too noisy."

Together they got up and went for a better look. Chlorine was already at the front door.

"It's Jay," Rick said. "Delivering groceries."

"Oh, no," Nellie groaned. She hadn't seen him since she'd gotten him fired from Petrone's. She wasn't sure she wanted to see him now, either.

She slipped back into the kitchen before Jay reached the door. Chlorine's voice got muffled, then louder.

Nellie stood in the corner, listening, her back to the wall. *Please let Jay take his money and turn around and leave.*

It was one of those prayers not answered the way Nellie planned. About as soon as she'd gotten herself wedged into the corner, Chlorine came into the room, practically towing Jay and the groceries behind her.

He carried a box and two bags piled in front of his face, and Chlorine had to tell him where the table was, so he could set them down. Nellie had started tiptoeing toward the door when Jay looked her way.

"Hi." She felt her face go red.

"Hey." Jay didn't seem to react at all, but then there was no way he could know Nellie was who'd called the police on him.

"Here's your money, young man." Chlorine fished bills from a worn-out blue wallet and counted them. She checked the coin section. "And here's something for you, too. Merry Christmas."

"Thanks."

"I'd like to offer you a cup of tea," Chlorine started to say. Jay backed hastily toward the kitchen door, zipping his jacket over a Superette Dollar Days T-shirt.

"No, that's okay, ma'am. I've got to get back." He ducked through the doorway.

"Excuse me," Nellie muttered to Chlorine and followed Jay.

He'd paused in the living room to answer a question from Rick. "Nah, that's okay. I'll call sometime."

Jay opened the door and turned up his collar. Nellie swallowed. She knew what she had to do, even though it made her knees wobble.

"Go help Chlorine put the groceries away, okay?" she asked Rick and Peggy. "I'll be right back."

She ignored Peggy's raised eyebrows. If she talked about this, she'd chicken out.

Nellie pulled open the door and slipped outside, shivering in her shirtsleeves against the cold. The sun was sinking into the horizon.

Jay was already sliding across the yard toward his car. Its purple shape gleamed like a forgotten eggplant against the drab mud and slush.

Catching onto the porch rail, Nellie swallowed her thudding heartbeat. "Jay?" Her voice disappeared into the racket of dogs' barking.

"Jay!" she called more loudly, shivering as the wind shifted.

He turned with his hand on the car door, looking surprised. "Yeah?"

Nellie hurried down the steps and picked her way across the yard. "Jay, I just—" She stopped a few feet from him, hugging herself against the cold. She was really shaking now, maybe more from nerves than the raw wind.

"Jay, I'm sorry. I wanted to say how sorry I—"

He shrugged. "It's okay. Not your fault." He opened the car door.

"No!" Nellie followed him. "No, it is my fault. Jay, I'm the one who—"

He stopped and stared at her. She swallowed.

"I called the police, but only because you had all that mail in your car. I mean, not that we were snooping, but what happened was, we were in the parking lot at Petrone's. And your lights were on."

Jay still stared at her. Looking down as she rubbed her frozen fingers together, Nellie told the whole story.

She glanced back up. Jay was tugging at the little ponytail on top of his head, as if he were thinking. A scowl darkened his face.

"Oh, Jay, I'm sorry," Nellie repeated. "I never meant to cause—"

He focused on her then, the frown melting. "That's okay. My life's rotten, anyway."

He laughed, but not happily. "Wouldn't you know it? I *never* leave my lights on—I can see them against the wall in front of me when I park. So wouldn't you know the one time I do, there's

154

stolen mail in the car?"

Jay shook his head at the questioning look on Nellie's face. "I don't know how it got there. But there it is. And I leave the lights on. Probably thinking about Shelley and old Big Foot."

"What? I mean, who?"

"Deke, the cook," he said. "He's a real pain in the neck."

Jay climbed halfway into the car and gave Nellie a crooked smile. It made him look a lot nicer. "Don't worry about it, kid. It was just one of those things."

Nellie smiled back. "Thanks."

Jay shrugged. "No big deal. See ya." He got in and closed the door.

She stood and watched him back the car, lurching down the driveway. A thought had begun to turn through her brain. It wasn't clear yet, but something was swimming toward the surface.

"Big Foot," Nellie mouthed. It was another name for Sasquatch.

She remembered how Deke had tripped Jay and Jay had snapped something about big feet. But were they really? Or was it just an expression?

She frowned, trying to remember. If Deke really did have big feet, he could've left that big footprint by the Lucky Clover mailboxes.

Chlorine's dogs had left tracks in the mud and snow in the front yard. The melting had spread them so they looked like a bunch of bears had been prowling. Deke's print would've spread, too.

Deke—the thought intrigued her. She'd like it to be Deke. He was so nasty, she could enjoy sending him to jail.

Nellie hurried back up the porch steps. It made a lot of sense. Deke was buying Shelley presents. And who'd be in a better position to plant the evidence in Jay's car?

She could *see* Deke doing it. He'd be snickering the whole time. In fact, she could see him stealing the mail just so he could stick Jay with the blame. He might have even picked the Lucky Clover, knowing Jay would be seen in the area around the time of the theft.

And if he'd seen them find the stolen envelopes, why else wouldn't he take the pleasure of reporting Jay to the police himself? Maybe because he couldn't afford any attention from the police, either.

As she pushed the door open to the nose-piercing smell of Chlorine's tea, her heart sank. Deke might be the thief, all right. But how would she ever prove it?

24

A Trap for a Crook

Peggy came from Chlorine's kitchen with a tissue to her nose. She sneezed mightily.

"God bless you."

"Are you ready?" Peggy's voice was pleading. Nellie scowled.

"Well, you don't need to look like that," Peggy told her. "We've been here for hours."

"No—I mean, I'm sorry. I'm not mad at you. It's just that when I saw the tissue I remembered."

"What?"

Though she could hear Rick and Chlorine talking in the other room, Nellie lowered her voice. "The handkerchief. And the sachet. I think I know who stole the mail—or I thought I did."

"Huh?"

"I just don't know how the handkerchief fits."

Peggy blew her nose. "I think it's just an ordinary hankie. It's not one of a kind, you know."

"I know." Nellie chewed at her lower lip, then

stopped, realizing how chapped and sore it was getting.

Rick stuck his head through the doorway. "You guys soon ready?"

Nellie nodded. "I'll call my mom," Peggy said.

Nellie took a deep breath. She'd leveled with Jay and it hadn't killed her.

She found Chlorine folding grocery bags in the kitchen. Rick went to collect their jackets from the coat-tree near the back door.

"Chlorine?"

"Yes, Nellie."

"I just wondered—I bought some of your stuff at the auction, and there was a hankie. And a sachet. They were like new. And I wondered about them. Maybe it was a mistake, or. . . ." She let her voice trail off.

Chlorine reached up to straighten her bent red feather. It seemed an almost embarrassed gesture.

The hand stopped and Chlorine looked out at Nellie from under it. "Did young Mike head on home?"

Nellie nodded. "Awhile ago."

Chlorine's black lashes fluttered down like a pair of weary bats. "May as well say the truth," she sighed. "But don't say anything to the boy—please?"

"Of course," Nellie promised.

"I just don't have any need for that fancy stuff around here." She waved a hand at the room.

Rick, holding a double armload of coats,

raised his eyebrows at Nellie from the back hall-way.

"Mike gave you that stuff?" Nellie asked.

Chlorine nodded. "He's such a good-hearted boy. But I need what little money I can scrape together more than any present. And really—" Chlorine looked from Nellie to Rick and then to Peggy, who'd appeared in the other doorway. "It really was the thought that counts. It meant more to me that the boy wanted to give me a gift than any gift itself could have meant."

Nellie nodded. "I think I know what you mean."

"You won't tell him?"

"Of course not."

Chlorine grinned. "Thanks. You sure are good kids." She threw an arm around Nellie's shoulder and hugged.

"I wish I could show my appreciation somehow." Chlorine looked thoughtfully around the room. "Wait now. I've got it."

She released Nellie from her crushing hug and swooped across the room, shedding red pinfeathers. She flung open the cupboard above the stove and pulled out a big mayonnaise jar full of what looked like scraps of burnt paper.

She plunked it into Nellie's hand. "Some of my special tea! Especially good for colds, flu, and dyspepsia."

At Nellie's look of dismay, Chlorine added, "I'm sorry I just have the one jar to spare right now. But I think there's enough for all three of you if you divide it into smaller jars when you get home. Truly, you don't want to use too much," she cautioned. "It's quite powerful."

"Wow." Nothing else would come out of Nellie's mouth.

"Thank you," Peggy said. "But you won't want to run out of tea yourself. And we don't expect anything for helping out."

Grinning, Chlorine waved an airy hand. "Oh, I know you didn't, you lamb. But I want to give you something. You just enjoy it, now."

Peggy's mom decided, like Chlorine, that Nellie, Rick, and Peggy deserved a reward for their hard work. Luckily, her idea of a reward was a large pizza and not herbal tea.

Sitting crosslegged on the Penwicks' game room floor, Nellie cautiously rearranged hot cheese on top of her pizza. "Honestly, one of you guys better take that tea," she pleaded. "She listed her ingredients on the side, for goodness sake. If Mom gets hold of that, she's liable to make us a big batch. I could end up drinking that stuff till I go away to college."

"Exactly," Peggy told her. "It'll be more appreciated at your house."

"Funny," Nellie griped.

"I'll take it." Rick scooped up the jar and studied Chlorine's label. "With luck, Mom'll give it to Billy next time he plays sick on a school day."

Nellie scratched a stockinged foot. "You're welcome to it."

"Hey, guys, seriously. Do you think Mike stole the mail?" Peggy asked. "Since he had the hankie and the sachet?"

Nellie shook her head. "I just can't see him doing that. And how'd he get to those other places the mail was stolen? Or leave stuff in Jay's car? No—it was Deke the sneak."

"Mike probably just picked those couple things up off the ground," Rick agreed. "He was hanging around the edge of the crowd that day."

Peggy made a face. "I hate to think of him stealing stuff—even a couple little things like that."

"Me, too." Nellie frowned. "He probably just saw them and thought of Chlorine. He's kind of a lost puppy—just wants somebody to love him."

No one said anything for a while, but finally Peggy threw a twig into the glowing fireplace and asked, "If it *is* Deke, what next? We don't have any proof. Or any way of getting some."

"I know." Nellie flopped face down on the rug. "If there was any evidence, he dumped it all on Jay."

"Maybe the police made a casting of his big footprint," Rick said. "They could compare that to his shoes."

Nellie rolled her head sideways to grimace at him. "Like I should call the police *again*? I don't think so. They probably have my name above the phone with a warning sign: 'Don't Take Tips from This Person.' "

Rick grinned. "Oh, but this is a good tip."

"Sure. I just say, 'Officer, please arrest Deke because I don't like him, and Jay called him 'Big Foot.' "

"Oh well, when you put it that way."

"So how *are* we going to prove it?" Peggy interrupted.

"I don't know." Nellie sat up and hugged her knees, resting her chin on them. "Let's think about this."

"We could trick him," Peggy suggested.

"How?"

"Well. . . ." Peggy thought. "Maybe by getting him to reveal something only the mail thief would know."

"And what, pray tell, would that be? You watch too much TV." Rick snorted. "If only the mail thief knows it, how are *we* supposed to know?"

"It was just an idea," Peggy said with dignity.

Nellie thought harder. "Well, on TV—" she began. Catching the look in Rick's eye, she waved him off. "I know, I know. But on TV, the bad guy will have you cornered and he figures since he's planning to eliminate you anyway, he has nothing to lose, so—"

"He confesses," Rick concluded. "So all we need to do is sneak into Petrone's after hours and get Deke to come at us with a pizza cutter."

"Cute idea," Nellie muttered. "Well, maybe we could get him to confess some other way."

"Like how?" Peggy asked.

"Bragging, maybe."

Rick looked doubtful. "I can see him bragging, but about this? To *us*? He's not stupid, is he?"

"Maybe not that stupid," Nellie reluctantly conceded. "He might tell a friend, I guess."

"That leaves us out," Peggy said.

"And Jay," Rick added. "Definitely."

Nellie brightened. "Wait! I do know who he'd tell."

"Who?" Peggy asked.

"Shelley!"

The others just looked at her, so Nellie prompted them. "Right?"

"I guess so," Peggy finally said. "But we don't know her."

Nellie waved an impatient hand. "So what? We're not the ones in trouble. Jay is. And Shelley really loves him. She'd do it for him. I know she would."

"You're right," Rick said. "And I do know her—a little bit." He looked at his watch. "Let's see if we can go talk to her right now."

25

Shelley

Unfortunately, Peggy's mom couldn't understand the need for another trip to Petrone's—not when they'd just finished a large pizza. Nellie's hint that there was always room for pizza didn't impress her one bit.

They'd just about decided to try it next weekend when Nellie's dad came to pick her up. "I can drop you off, too, Rick, if you don't mind an extra stop on the way home."

"Thanks, that'd be great."

It turned out Dad wanted to stop at Petrone's for calzones. "Danny had a craving," he explained.

Danny wasn't well-equipped in the tooth department, so Nellie knew who had the craving. "Ever since Dad discovered calzones, he can't quit," she whispered. "They even come vegetarian, so it's like the greatest thing that's happened in his life since grainburgers."

As they pulled into Petrone's lot, Nellie held out a hand for money. "We'll run in for you."

Rick scrambled out behind her. "How are you going to talk to Shelley if Deke's there?"

"I hope he is," Nellie told him. "I want to get a look at those feet. After that, I'm not sure," she admitted.

Rick pulled open the door and Nellie walked in, quickly scanning the room. Shelley was serving a pizza in one corner and Deke was in the kitchen.

"Here." She shoved the money into Rick's hand. "Could you pick up Dad's calzone and check out those feet for me? You ought to be able to get a look from the take-out window."

"Okay." Rick gave her a questioning look.

"I'm going to talk to Shelley."

Nellie angled her way between tables to catch Shelley before she could walk back to the kitchen. Glancing that way, she saw that Deke was busy sprinkling cheese.

Nellie slipped into a chair with her back to the kitchen. Shelley rushed past. "I'll be with you in a minute."

"No, Shelley!"

Shelley turned. "Huh?"

"I need to talk to you. It's important," Nellie hissed.

Shelley studied her. "Do I know you?"

Nellie shook her head. "Not really. But I'm a friend of—well, I'm kind of here on behalf of Jay. Can you pretend to take an order?"

Shelley raised her eyebrows, but she stepped nearer. "I guess. But if the cook sees me, he's going to wonder what happened to your order."

"Are you allowed a rest room break?"

Shelley nodded.

"All right. I'm going back there. Follow me in about a minute, okay? I need to talk to you about something that could get Jay out of trouble."

"Really?" Shelley looked doubtful.

"Honest," Nellie promised. "I think I may know who stole all that mail, and how to prove it, but I'll need your help."

"Well, all right." She still looked as if she didn't think Nellie was a very likely source of help, but at least there had been a brief glimmer of hope in her eyes.

Nellie scooted toward the back hallway. When she passed Rick, he casually spread his hands below counter level.

Yes! She knew the gesture meant "big, big feet." Nellie kept going, barely glancing at Rick as he seemed to keep his attention behind the counter, focused on the progress of Dad's calzone.

The ladies room was big enough for two people, but it was empty. Nellie slipped inside and waited, heart thudding.

She caught a glimpse of herself in the mirror and shuddered—windburned cheeks, dirt from her day of cleaning, and hair that stood up like the fur on a wet dog who'd just shaken himself.

Using her fingers, Nellie raked down the hair.

No wonder Shelley didn't have much confidence in her.

There was nothing she could do about the dirt on her clothes, but she dampened a paper towel and scrubbed a couple smudges from her face. Just then the door opened. Shelley.

"This has got to be quick. I've got customers."

"Okay." Nellie drew a breath and began reeling off her theory about Deke.

Shelley's lips thinned and a frown settled across her eyes. "You might be right," she said. "Deke would do it just to get Jay in trouble, even if *he* didn't make a cent from it himself."

"And so he could get in good with you," Nellie pointed out. Shelley was the kind of girl who'd be too modest to mention that guys fought over her.

"What I think," Nellie told her, "is that Deke would tell you what he did, if he thought you'd be impressed. It's about the only way I can think of that he'd get caught. Unless he tries stealing more mail."

Shelley twisted her long, black ponytail. "Deke may not have done it, you know."

Nellie didn't want to think about that. "Will you at least try, though?"

Shelley flipped the ponytail back over her shoulder. "Okay. For Jay."

26

In Hot Water at Petrone's

"Hey, this is actually fun." Nellie sloshed water across Petrone's kitchen tile with the big mop. "Maybe I'll be a janitor for a living."

"Anyone who ever saw your house would never offer you the job," Peggy told her. "No offense."

"None taken."

While Nellie mopped and Peggy wiped counters and tables with disinfectant cleaner, Rick was being towed across the dining room carpet by an enormous sweeper. It growled like it was competing in the County Fair tractor pull, so Nellie and Peggy had to holler.

Nellie glanced at Deke, who was cleaning up the ovens and cooking supplies, then at Shelley, who was closing out the register.

It was only 6:00 p.m., but already dark outside. Petrone's business was slow on Sundays, and it closed early.

Putting her face close to Nellie's ear, Peggy

hissed, "Lucky Rick's Aunt Connie had the flu."

Nellie shook her head. "Not for her. Besides, she said she really was better."

"The important thing," Peggy said, stealing a glance at Deke and Shelley, "is that she said okay when Rick offered to do her cleanup. That makes three more witnesses for Shelley."

"I know. My parents are going to wonder if I'm going for a Girl Scout merit badge, helping Chlorine yesterday and doing this today."

"Well, I'm done," Peggy announced.

"Almost," Nellie said, taking a final swipe at the floor before putting her mop through the wringer at the top of the bucket.

As they collected their cleaning supplies, the vacuum cleaner coughed to silence. Nellie's ears rang.

"Well, I think we're through here," Rick told Shelley.

She smiled. Nellie wondered if there was a nervous tremble to her lips, but her voice sounded natural. "Thanks, kids. After you put your stuff away, you can go out front or back. We didn't set the burglar alarm yet."

The janitor's closet was almost like a small room, with storage shelves overhead bulging with paper towels, cleansers, and stick-on deodorizers. Brooms, mops, and buckets stood along the walls.

Grunting, Nellie tipped her mop bucket over the low slop sink. Peggy and Rick stowed their supplies, then Rick put a finger over his lips.

169

"I'll get the coats and open and shut the back door, okay?" he whispered. "You wait here."

Nellie nodded, hugging her arms against a shiver of excitement. Peggy rubbed at her nose as if the aroma of dustrags and chemicals was tickling her allergies.

The back door opened, then closed with a thud and click. Seconds later, Rick slipped inside the closet, hugging a double armload of jackets and trailing Peggy's green scarf.

"I hate to do this, but we need to kill the lights," he said, dumping their coats in the corner.

"Okay." Nellie swallowed, trying not to remember how she hated small, dark places. After all, the light would show beneath the door, and they didn't want Deke to come in to turn it off.

But as she reached for the switch, Peggy grabbed her hand. "Can we leave the door ajar?"

Nellie raised eyebrows at Rick.

"I guess so," he said, shrugging. "We may need to, so we can hear."

Nellie reached for the switch again, but Peggy was faster. "Uh, what if they push it shut? Will we be locked in?"

The hair on the back of Nellie's neck prickled. She hadn't thought of that.

"We'd better try it," she said, starting to push open the door.

Suddenly Rick blocked her, putting one hand to her mouth as he hit the light switch with the other.

Deke's voice was very near. "They're gone," he said from the hallway. "You about done, Shel?"

Nellie heard a reply from the kitchen but couldn't make out the words. She grabbed Rick's hand in the darkness and squeezed.

Deke's voice moved back toward the kitchen and dining room. "You wanna go someplace?"

"Oh, I don't know, Deke." Shelley's voice was clearer. She must have walked back to the register. "I feel a little funny—you know, about Jay."

Deke snorted. "That loser? He can't even steal a few envelopes without leaving the evidence sit in his car."

"That *was* stupid, wasn't it?"

Deke's chuckle fell into a brief silence.

"The guy finally shows some ambition, then blows it," she said. "I'm probably better off without him. I never knew how to tell him to get lost."

"I can tell him for you," Deke offered. "Anytime you want."

"I wonder why he'd be so stupid?" Shelley said. "Anyone with a brain would've dumped that stuff the first chance he got."

Deke laughed again. "No, baby, you know what someone with a brain does? He unloads the evidence on somebody else."

A long moment of silence, then Shelley chuckling. "Oh, Deke, you *didn't*?"

He didn't deny it. Was that a confession? Nellie hesitated, agonizing. If they waited too long, they'd be caught sneaking out—or worse yet, locked in.

171

"You didn't really think dummy had the guts to pull something like that off, did you?" Deke's voice was gloating.

Rick decided for Nellie, giving her a little push toward the door. Softly she pushed it a bit wider and peeked.

The coast was clear. Taking big steps, she headed for the restaurant's rear door. Rick followed, with Peggy and the coats.

Nellie's heartbeat crashed in her ears and she could barely breathe. Turning the lock, it occurred to her to wonder if Rick had locked it earlier, when he'd faked their exit.

Too late. The pulsing scream of the burglar alarm answered her question.

27

No More Mysteries— Right?

"Hey, what's going on there?"

Nellie spun wildly to see Deke. His fists were clenched, and he was glaring at the three of them. Behind him stood Shelley, white-faced.

Before she could think of anything to say, he lunged forward, catching Rick and Peggy by their collars. "You little creeps! Hold it right there."

He only had two hands. Nellie pushed open the door and plunged through the opening into the cold outside air, the shriek of the security alarm at her back.

Help! She had to get help!

Running blindly into the parking lot, Nellie crashed into a solid form. "Wh—?" she gasped, looking up.

Holding onto her arms, Jay looked blankly down at her. "What happened?"

"The burglar alarm. Deke stole the mail," she

puffed. "Shelley. He grabbed Peggy and Rick."

He shoved her aside and ran to the door. Still gasping, Nellie watched him. She knew she hadn't made any sense.

Mrs. Hostetler came running down the outside steps leading to their apartment, feet clanging on the steel risers. Her eyes were big, scared circles in a pale face. "Nellie, what happened? Are Rick and Peggy all right?"

Before Nellie could answer, a Begg City police cruiser pulled into the lot. "What happened?" the first officer asked, getting out of the car.

Quickly Nellie explained. She was still talking when the officers told her to stay put and headed for the restaurant door.

* * *

The school library was quiet. It was study hall, but Nellie wasn't studying.

"What are you writing?" Peggy whispered.

Self-consciously, Nellie covered her paper. "Nothing."

At her friend's hurt look, Nellie sighed. "Oh, all right." She moved her arm away so Peggy could see.

"New Year's resolutions?" Peggy clamped a hand over her mouth and looked down when the librarian frowned at them.

Nellie slid the page so Peggy could see.

"Don't be so suspicious," Peggy read softly, then grinned. "Give me a break!"

174

"I mean it," Nellie whispered earnestly while her eyes darted toward the librarian's desk. "First Jay, then Chlorine. Even Mike. And all they needed was somebody to care about them. No more mysteries."

"Sure." Peggy stifled a snort. "But you *were* right about Deke, so you ended up helping Jay. And Chlorine, too. And you solved the Big Foot mystery."

Nellie hesitated, remembering the figure in the woods. She wasn't at all sure that Deke—and Mike's slipper—constituted the entire local Big Foot population. "Maybe. But there are still 'more mysteries in heaven and on earth' than I'm ever going to figure out in this lifetime. And all they do is get me into trouble."

Peggy just shook her head. "If you stop looking for them, they'll just come after you. Kind of like me and the mold spores," she added, hastily blowing her nose as the librarian glared in their direction.

The Author

Susan Kimmel Wright would rather read than sleep at night. She especially loves mysteries. Susan has learned that life really is full of mysteries, and that wonderful and amazing things do happen to ordinary people if we just look for them.

Susan was born and grew up in the mountains of western Pennsylvania. She later became a lawyer as well as a mom and writer. Susan and her husband, Dave, and children, Tony, Kika, and Daisy, live in an old farmhouse on a country road near Bridgeville, along with enough animals to keep a zookeeper busy. They attend Zion Lutheran Church & School, where Susan is a member of the Board of Christian Education.

You may write to Susan in care of Herald Press. She'd love to hear from you.